Charge it to the Game

Keaidy Selmon

OTHER BOOKS BY KEAIDY SELMON

Charge it to the Game 2: Tammy's Story

Charge it to the Game 3: Three Sides to Every Story

Charge it to the Game 4: Pride Comes B4 Destruction (Coming 2021)

Somewhere Between Love & Misunderstanding

The Chronicles of a Love Addict

When a Woman's Fed Up

She Fell in Love With a Boss

Shut Up & Finish Your Book Already

DEDICATION

To my motivation for greatness (Khloe and Isaiah): May you guys
never forget that you can do ALL things through Christ who
strengthens you. Keep that scripture in your heart always – no matter
how things look in front of you.
Love,
-Mom

LexxiKhan Presents Publishing
www.LexxiKhanPresents.com

Ordering Information:
Quantity sales. Special discounts are available on quantity purchases by corporations, associations, schools and others. For details, contact the publisher at the address above.

This book contains an excerpt from the next installment in the Charge It to the Game series. It may be edited or deleted prior to actual publication.

ISBN: 978-0-9600635-0-5

MESSAGE FROM THE AUTHOR

From the bottom of my heart, thank you so much for your love and support. Writing an urban fiction novel was something I only dreamed of doing for almost a decade. The fact that I'm now not only doing it, but I'm encouraging others to follow their dreams also is an amazing feeling. Because of your support, you are helping to make the lives of our future generation of leaders easier. To find out more information and how you can help the cause to win back our youth, visit: Keaidy.com

This book does not glamorize selling/using drugs, committing murders/crimes, or anything else that is a part of the street life. Because all though we call it a game, no one wins. Before you make the foolish decision to 'play,' make sure you consider a very important question. How much would you risk if what you lost you had to Charge it to the Game?

ACKNOWLEDGMENTS

Thank you mom for never giving up on me. Your love and strength motivates me to be a better woman every day. Thank you for teaching me about accountability and responsibility. Like you said it would happen, I hated it then, but I appreciate you because of it today.

Thanks pops for always buying mad copies! Life got much easier once I admitted I didn't know everything, and I actually listened to the things you were really saying to me. The advice you give is priceless. I love you.

I want so say a huge thank you to my sister who has always been my inspiration to write. I can't wait for the story inside of you to explode into a project that will blow even your mind, kid. It's because of you I ever took writing seriously. Your natural ability to manipulate regular words into intricate stories and poems made me step up my game. Your word play is genius. Thanks.

PROLOGUE

I didn't follow the original 10 crack commandments because I made my own rules. Number 1, keep both heads where they're supposed to be because hoes equal drama, and after a decade of success – I don't need none. My mama named me Kyle, and my name holds just as much weight in these Orlando streets as the product I move.

It was 2010, and I was young with everything I thought I could have ever wanted. I was 22 with a brand new Dodge Charger, and money was never a problem for me. Yeah, I thought I had it all. Well, that was until I met her.

Tamia Santiago can move more product than most men I know. As a matter of fact, I had to step my game up because of her. When her orders got larger, so did mine. Because of her, I realized "owning my city" was nothing. I deserved the world, and it was mine the moment I decided to own it.

She's smart, successful, and has no problem pulling out her tool. She's a college student, full-time employee, and the owner of a successful cosmetics line that she uses to clean up her drug money. She's nothing to play with. She does her thang, and she makes it look easy.

I had always been the type to rep money over bitches, but it was only because I never met anyone worth more than money, knew how to make her own, and helped me get more of it. Words out of her mouth sounded like butter, and to back up everything – she walked the talk. If she said it - she did it. If she promised you something – you could take it to the bank. She never made empty threats or promises. What man in his right mind wouldn't want a fine, loyal, ambitious Latina with a mean curve game?

I usually didn't invest my personal time trying to get to know women. Time is money to me, and every woman I've ever known has been a waste of it – even my mama. Like every gamble, I knew there was a risk for trying to deal with someone like her, but I just had to see if it was worth it.

I remember the day I met her like it was yesterday. I walked into Studio 167, where Jason was making a beat. He owned the studio and had an ear for music, so he did his thing. He never crossed me, and over the years, we had helped each other through many situations. He was an ally when the streets got hot for me. I didn't even have to ask; he just stepped in and helped me out. He didn't even want anything for it. No one had ever done that for me before. I never had a reason to question his loyalty, but I'm no dummy. You can't trust anyone, so you always have to stay on your toes.

Like I was saying, I walked into the studio, and he was making a beat. I had his shit in my duffel bag, ready to make the serve. Since I had plans that night, I was only going to drop it and go, but she was there. Because I didn't know who she was or why she was there, I had to find out.

I cut my eyes at Jason, waiting for him to explain, but before he could speak up, she used that as an opportunity to say something.

"Hey, it's nice to finally meet you. My bad about just poppin' up on you without warning or a proper introduction, but you know how this game can go."

I looked back at Jason.

"She's good, K.Y. I worked for her father for decades before I moved down here and started this. Niggas who lived the life I did for as long as I have never make it this far. I wouldn't keep anyone around that I couldn't trust. Shorty puts in work, and she loyal. Trust me, she's good.

I cut my eye back at her on the leather couch. She had to be around 5'6 and had the longest, prettiest legs I had ever seen. Her caramel complexion was blemish and mark-free, from her face down to the manicured toes in her sandals. She sure looked good, but mad bitches out here look good. That doesn't mean I should be rocking with them.

I walked in anyway and decided to join her on the couch.

"What's your name," I asked her once I was able to look directly into her eyes at eye level.

"It's Tamia, but everyone calls me Tammy. If it makes you feel more comfortable about the situation, we've already been doing business together for quite some time. I just had to see if I could trust you," she replied in some heavy up north accent.

Something about her energy told me she was legit. I put my duffle bag on the floor and relaxed a little more. Once Jason saw we were talking business, he put on his headphones and went back to work.

"The old guy just wants to retire. I don't want to continue to make him do my dirty work when I can handle it myself. I just want us to continue the smooth relationship without the need of my middle man," she continued.

I couldn't hold it in. I had to laugh. Sure, females thought they were about that life, but it's only cause they were trying to impress some nigga. These hoes don't really care about the game. They just care about the perks that come with fast money.

"That's cute," I said once I got a hold of my laughter. "If this is your order for real, then what's in the bag?"

"It's two pounds and a plate. Can I have my shit now, or would you like to continue being embarrassed in this dance?

She was feisty. I liked that shit.

"Just chill, shawty. A nigga just wanna make sure you good. Dat's it."

"Do you call any of these niggas you serve shawty?"

I was caught off guard with her question, but she never really gave me enough time to answer it.

"I bet you don't, so don't do that shit with me either. Keep it professional, so I can get Beast out of the equation, or I can take my business somewhere else," she snapped.

"I hear you. I won't do it again. We good."

I wanted to just change the subject, so I put the bag in front of her. The fight in her was turning me on, but I couldn't mess with my money just because I enjoyed the pistol in her.

"It's all there. You can check it if you want."

Without any hesitation, she grabbed the scale. She didn't trust me either.

I'm not going to lie. Watching her weight and bag out some of her shit got me in my head thinking a little bit. She was fine as fuck. I wondered if she was that direct in bed too. I would love to turn her over and teach her how to follow directions. Men clearly let her get away with a lot because she looks good. Shit, I'm not one of them.

"My man here is going to give you the money for this."

She said just as I was imagining what it would be like to bend her over this couch. I heard what she said, she wanted it and was going to give me the money, but it wasn't the whole amount. I can't remember how much it was that she was trying to play me with, but I wasn't going to let that happen.

"I don't give credit. Either pay me the whole thing, or we don't have a deal." *Oh, I would love to break you down*, I thought to myself as she cut her eye at me.

Instead of being intimidated by the fact that I didn't cave like most men would, I guess she thought it was funny. She started chuckling like a was a comedian telling her jokes.

"I wasn't asking for credit because I don't need any. I realize that you finally met me, but I'm not new to this – at all. You can overcharge those small-time dealers you mess with daily for a quick buck, or you can think like the businessman I know you are and make some real money with me.

Her confident gaze never wavered. I didn't like discounting anything. I didn't even give discounts to my mama, so what I look like practically giving my shit away? She was fine and feisty, though, so I figured I'd hook her up this time. I wanted to see if she was actually about that life.

"Aight. Just consider it my peace offering so you can keep this hostile attitude of yours in check. If we've been working together all of this time, it don't make sense to ruin a good thing, right?"

"You know something? I'm really looking forward to doing business with you more often. I love a man who isn't afraid to make a little investment."

She stood up to leave after putting her product into a couple shopping bags.

"I appreciate the hookup, Beast," she said as she lightly touched his shoulder.

"Stop calling me that, yo. I told you I'm going legit. I don't go by that down here."

"Whatever you say," she replied nonchalantly. "You know, I think you should reconsider that. It doesn't make any sense to not be true to who you really are."

"K.Y. I look forward to seeing you again real soon," she said as she shot me a glimpse of her beautiful smile. "Have a beautiful day, kings. Ciao." She sashayed out the door and left me with a million questions I couldn't ask while she was still there.

"Nigga, where you been hidin' her at," I asked as I put my scale and shit back in my duffle bag.

"I ain't been hiding nothing. The fuck kinda question is that?"

"I'm just saying why you ain't bring her by earlier. That's really who I've been working with?"

"Let me find out Tee got your ass open like that already," he responded with a laugh.

"Come on, dude. Let's be serious. You know I ain't open like that for nobody. I just wanna know. Who is she?"

"That's Tee. She just officially moved down here a little while ago. That's why you haven't met her yet. Real shit, you might just want to forget about that one. Her father has he so spoiled that she is not going to deal with just any little boy.
I ain't trying to play you fam, but you don't got a chance with a shorty like that. Just keep doing what you do – focus only on the business and leave her alone personally."

"Oh yeah, bruh, so you really wanna act like I'm some lil' nigga who hasn't been doing his thang for damn near 10 years? I can have any female I want because they know I've been on my shit since I was only 12."

"Nigga, I know this. Even though we just started out as me buying from you, I look at you as my boy, so I'm doing you a favor by giving you this information. Stay in your league, fam. Stick with the broads you're used to."

"Fuck that. I appreciate your advice, but I might actually have to break my rule and spend a little time picking her brain. I'll be good. You've never known me to be a dog to these bitches. I hardly give them any play to begin with." We both laughed cause we both knew it was right.

"You've been doing a good job of keeping both heads where they belong. That's why I believe you've had as much success as you've had throughout the years. I love Tee because I know if anyone knows the game – it's her. She's run with some real thorough breads, so I know she knows her shit. Just be careful.

Her orders have been picking up, which means I know you're about to make some major cash if you keep working with her. I just don't want you to lose focus and miss some opportunities that can really get you to the kind of money you deserve to be making.

I know for a fact that if anyone can get you to the status you want to be on, it's her. I also know that she can be a pistol with her mouth and isn't afraid to pop off with it. If she feels disrespect in any way, she'll cut every kind of relationship tie you have – even the business one.

No offense, she a smart businesswoman, but she's still a woman. It's rare, but occasionally she'll think with her heart. Don't make her put you in that position. Stay focused, man. "

The game had taught me many things. One thing I was sure of was in the opportunities I took. I never did anything my gut didn't tell me to do. Why? Because with this type of career, it's easy to lose it all over a wrong move. She just seemed worth it to me, so I had to do something about it. I had to ask myself something I hadn't really thought about in a minute, *"Kyle, how much would you risk if what you lost you had to **Charge it to the Game?**"*

CHAPTER ONE

It had been over three weeks since K.Y. met Tee in the studio, and he had not seen her again since. It was evident that she knew what she was doing with her product because her orders got larger. They were also coming in more frequently, but instead of dealing with him directly, she still had Jason setting up and finishing all of her deals.

"What the hell is up with your girl," K.Y. finally asked Jason as they were completing another order. "I've been dealing with you all of these years, and I've never given you prices this low. You bring this girl one time, and now I'm discounting every pound. If I go any lower, I'll be giving it to you at my price," he said, clearly frustrated. "Was this part of your master plan to get cheaper shit or somethin'," K.Y. asked his friend bluntly.

"In all the time we've been doing business together, when have you ever known me to try to hustle you? I don't move weight like that anymore; I just keep the product in the studio for my rappers under my label. Don't you get it that I'm going to be 40 years old this year? I can't live this kind of life forever. I'm finally starting to make some real money from this studio, and I can't let these streets fuck me up. The streets are not always as good as they have been to me, and it's about time that I thank Jah and keep it movin'. I promised her old man that I would help her get situated out here. Then, I would let her handle things on her own. Just be patient."

"Whatever, bruh, I just can't help but feel like I'm being played. Dis woman is moving more than 10 pounds a week, but I never see her out here in these streets."

7

"Unlike these broads you're used to, this girl has a job and is in college. She's just smart and selective about how she operates her business. If you're that anxious to see her, meet me tonight at the studio. She'll be there."

"Bet."

***

It was a quarter to midnight when K.Y finally got the text he had been hoping to see for weeks.

"She's here, but I'm not sure for how long," the text read.

K.Y. made sure to handle all of his business near the studio for that reason.

He pulled up in front of Jason's studio in downtown Orlando and checked the mirror to make sure he was good before stepping out of his vehicle. *Why am I doing all of this for a chick I've only met once,* he thought to himself. Then, he watched her walking out and immediately remembered why.

He jumped out of his car to help her because she looked like she needed it. She had been carrying a lot of bags and boxes, and he didn't want her to trip in those nice red bottoms she was wearing.

"Thank you, sir; I appreciate all of the help," she said in the tone that K.Y. had fantasized about several times since they first met.

"Ain't no need to be so formal, Tee. Don't you remember meeting me before?"

"Tee is a nickname reserved for family and close family friends, so you can call me Tammy. Of course, I remember meeting you," she replied, this time removing all of the sugar from her voice.

"My bad. I didn't know you could be so touchy on a nickname. In case you forgot, my name is Kyle. Everyone just calls me K.Y."

"I know. How could I forget the name of a man whose product didn't weigh out properly like it should have the last couple pounds I bought? You trying to get over on me?"

"Shit, I could say the same about you. How do you come around once and get a serious discount and feel like you can keep getting it when I'm not dealing with you directly?"

They finally reached her Toyota Camry, and she popped the trunk to put all of her items inside.

"Isn't money the motive? Why does it matter if you're getting my money from Jason or if you're getting it from me as long as you get it?"

8

"It matters cause I never give niggas the kind of discount that I'm givin' you."

She flashed him her signature sly side grin. "Beast already told me that you think I'm trying to get over on you, so clearly, I'm just going to have to show you how I operate. Leave your phone, any electronics, and your burner in the car. Take off your shirt now."

K.Y. thought to question her requests, but the amount of emphasis she gave on each direction let him know that nothing was really up for debate. She handed him a Ralph Lauren Polo from one of her bags in the trunk.

"Now, take off your pants."

He glanced around to make sure no one was watching, and then he quickly did as he was told.

I'm not sure your exact size, but these should fit you." She handed him a pair of well-pressed khaki pants and a belt. Everything seemed to fit him perfectly. "That blue really compliments your skin well," she said as she smoothed out his shirt. "Just because you're from the hood doesn't mean that you have to make it so obvious all the time.

I have Beast do all of my deals with you because I have a reputation to protect. I moved away from home because I was tired of all of the drama that the street life comes with. But no matter how much you try to change, you can't change who you really are.

Thanks to my past, the street life is where I'm most comfortable, so I can't leave it alone. Instead, I just had to learn new rules and change up my game a little bit.

Now, go drop all your shit off in the car. Lock it up, and get in."

Without a word, he did as he was told.

"You didn't show this side of you before, but you're very bossy," he finally said once he was comfortable inside of her car. "I'm not sure how much I like it."

"Well, you're more than welcome to get your black ass off of my seats and find something less productive to do. I'm not forcing you to do anything." She waited a minute before she started her car. "I'm going to assume by your silence and the fact that you're still in that chair that you like it more than you want to believe," she chuckled.

"I'm not used to anyone talking to me this way – especially not a female."

"Get used to it. I get called much worse things than bossy but, of course, never directly to my face. Anyway, I feel like I've done enough talking about myself. Tell me something about you."

"Dat all depends. What do you wanna know shawty?"

"For starters, I want to know why you can't address me by the name my parents gave me. My name is Tamia. It's not baby or shawty. You don't speak to any of your other business partners that way, so I don't want to hear it either," she said firmly. "How did you get started, and how long have you been doing this?"

"Well, *Tammy*," he said, emphasizing her name. "My mom was a single parent 'cause my no good ass daddy would rather be out here in dese streets making more babies than taking care of the ones he already had. I'm the oldest of 3 kids, so I felt it was my job to step up and be the man of the house that my father wasn't. One of my uncles put me on as a runner at the age of 12. I've been doing my thang ever since."

"So where are they now?"

"I'd rather not talk about it. It's really personal."

"No problem. I'm really inquisitive, so I have a tendency to ask a lot of personal questions. You can always talk about it whenever you're ready."

Just as she had finished speaking, she parked her car in front of what seemed to be an abandoned building. "No offense, but I can't have you up in here embarrassing me. You have two options: you can wait very patiently out here, or you can come in, sit down, and shut up. When I say shut up, I mean it! I want you to remain absolutely mute and let me do all the talking. If anyone speaks to you, a simple nod would be a sufficient response."

Without speaking, he got out of the car to let he know she was understood.

"Can you grab the items from the trunk quickly and quietly, please? I have a lot of moves to make before the sun comes up, and I don't want to be in here longer than we need to be."

He did as he was told, but he was in complete shock as to what he found when they entered the old building.

A beautiful exotic woman greeted them as soon as they entered, wearing only some peep-toe stilettos. Everything on this woman was beautiful, from her head down to her pedicured toes.

"Ms. Santiago, you're just in time! All of the party-goers were getting so anxious about your arrival."

"Mrs. Carter, you know I'm always on time, and I never aim to disappoint any of my clients. You look lovely this evening as always."

"Thank you, sweetheart, you look just as delicious as you have since I met you," Mrs. Carter said, not even trying to hide the fact that she was coming on to Tammy. "If you ever change your mind about females, I trust that you know exactly who you can call," she said, giving Tammy a wink.

"Believe me, if I did ever want to experiment with a woman, you would be the only one I could be curious enough to taste," Tammy replied seductively.

Mrs. Carter used her manicured nails to gently push some of Tammy's long curly hair back before sliding her fingers down her body to grab her hand. "Follow me."

It was hard for K.Y. not to get turned on by this side of Tammy. He watched both women as they walked hand in hand to some plush office in the front of the warehouse. Obviously, Mrs. Carter was an older woman, but she had the body that most women half of her age would pay to have. Even in her clothes, he could tell that if Tammy were also naked, she could give Mrs. Carter a clear run for her money. Both women had large breasts, slim waists, and hips so curvy they demanded full attention from every eye they walked by.

"Please have a seat," Mrs. Carter said once they were locked inside of her office.

"Mrs. Carter, this is a friend of mine. I'm showing him around the business because he is thinking of becoming a distributor of the products himself," Tammy said. "I've been saying forever that I want to expand, and he might just be the one to help me get it done."

"Well it's really nice to meet you, handsome. I've never had the chance to meet any of Tammy's people's, so it's a pleasure to finally do so."

K.Y. returned her greeting with a brief smile and nod.

"He's not much of a talker, I see," Mrs. Carter responded.

"No he's not. He prefers to sit back and just observe. I prefer it that way anyway."

Tammy began to place the bags in front of Mrs. Carter to give her some time to inspect her purchases. For the first time, K.Y finally caught a glimpse over the bags and boxes he had been carrying. Every box was a light pink color with a well-designed logo on the front. Each and every item that he had been carrying was labeled Beauty by Tammy. Not only was this girl street smart, but it seems like she was very business-oriented also. The more he got to know her, the more interested in her he became.

"Is it safe to fully inspect everything with him present," Mrs. Carter asked nervously.

"Yes, it is. I assure you that I would not have had him accompany me if I felt he would jeopardize either one of our businesses."

The woman removed the large box from the bag. Inside the box was a large makeup compact, but hidden inside, where the mirror should have been, was the stash she was looking for.

"Sir, I hope you don't mind, but I always like to test out my product before my purchase.

K.Y. simply shook his head and placed his palms up to let her know that he was okay with her doing whatever she needed to do.

Mrs. Carter crushed a few pills and used a hot pink straw to inhale the line through her nose. Afterward, she reclined in her oversized leather chair for a moment before she sat back up to acknowledge them.

"You never disappoint Ms. Santiago. Plus, it also helps that my dealer is so easy on the eyes. I hope you don't mind all of my clear attempts at you this evening, but you normally never come to see me so dressed up."

"Why would I take such beautiful words negatively when they are coming from a woman as sexy as you are," Tammy asked flirtatiously while eying the woman up and down. "I had a business meeting earlier this evening, and I never went home to change.

Tammy wore a sheer tan blouse that complimented her skin and a navy blue pencil skirt that sat exactly at her thin waist. The nude stilettos that she wore made her athletic legs look miles longer than they already did. Her natural hair fell down the middle of her back and was very silky and curly.

"I see. I usually only get the chance to see you in jeans and a tank top, but I would love to see this side of you more often.

Anyway, I have many clients inside waiting for me, so, unfortunately, I will have to cut this meeting short. How much will it be for my purchase this evening Ms. Santiago?"

Tammy replied, "Tonight's purchase is only $9800. I assume you're expecting a much smaller crowd this evening."

"A majority of my usual clients are out of town on vacation since the Fourth of July is right around the corner.

I'll be having another gathering this week, but it will be in a much more professional location. If you're free this Wednesday evening, you can join a few colleagues and me for dinner, and you can bring me another shipment of this size," she said. "I want the exact same products that you sold me tonight, so I'll just go ahead and pay for my order ahead of time.

K.Y had never seen a woman make almost $20,000 in less than twenty minutes without having to dance or take off a single item of her clothing.

"Just e-mail me the time and place, and I will be there." Tammy said as she finally got up.

"Well, sir, it was nice to meet you, but please follow me as I show you two out."

Once again, Ms. Carter grabbed Tammy's hand and led them to where they came in.

She opened the door to see K.Y out first. "It really was a pleasure meeting you even though you were so mute. Have a good night."

Before he could smile or nod to acknowledge her statement, she closed the door. K.Y. found himself in a strange area with a large amount of cash in his pocket and not a single weapon to protect him.

I don't like this shit, and this chick won't catch me slipping like this ever again. K.Y. paced around the front door a few times before finally deciding to walk over to the car. Before he even made it there, he felt someone following him.

"Yo," a homeless man called out to him. "You got a dollar I could get so I can catch the bus?"

K.Y had been selling drugs a long time, and this young bum's face looked all too familiar to him.

"Man, get the hell outta here. The bus stopped runnin' hours ago. I'm not gonna give you any of my money cause I know you'll come lookin' for something else from me later."

"It's only a dollar that I'm asking for, and I know you got it. That's what's wrong with the world today," the young man said before he started walking back to where he came from.

Several minutes after the bum disappeared, he heard the large door to the building open again. *It's about time. That chick has been in there for at least ten minutes.*

She unlocked the car from the door to give him a chance to get in first. He watched her as she walked back to the car, and even though it was dark, he could still manage to make out that she was fixing her clothes. *I know this chick didn't get her freak on while I was out here waiting. The least she could have done was let me watch if she was gonna fuck around.*

The moment she got to the car, and the light came on because her red lipstick wasn't as flawless as it was a few moments ago, confirmed his exact thoughts.

"You had me out here dealing with bums without shit to protect me while you were inside messing with that ol' ass lady. What the hell kind of business operation is that?"

She turned from the mirror she was looking at to fix her make-up to look at him directly.

"That old lady looks better than half of the broads you're pulling. Don't be mad because I don't even get down like that, but my bitches look better than yours. Jealousy doesn't really look cute on you," she said with a little chuckle.

"It's like you really don't know who you're dealing with. It's kind of annoying, but I kinda like it. You're good when you're with me, ok? That guy that walked over here was Jose. He's a young guy who made poor choices in his life. He knows my car, so he comes over here whenever he sees it. Unlike you, I usually give him a little something. Stop thinking you better than niggas just because you got some fancy piece of paper in your pocket.

Those motherfuckers never loved us, but we love them so much we'll kill for them. We love them so much, we'll even deny someone in need just to save the few dollars we do have.

I thought you really made money. If you made as much as you want to floss like you have, it shouldn't have killed you to help him out with a few bucks."

How can you honestly give him money when you know he's just going to use it to buy drugs later," K.Y. asked.

"I give him money for what he asks for. If he asks me for money for food or for the bus, then I am giving it to him for that purpose. We are all God's children, and it's our job to look out for one another. If he uses my money for something other than what he asked for, then he'll have to answer to God on judgment day. It's not up to me to judge him or the life he lives."

"I guess I never looked at it like that. I just think it's crazy to give someone money when I know what they are using it for."

"You THINK you know what they are using it for. I have watched people turn their lives around without a rehab facility or medicine to wean them off of anything. The business that we are in does more damage to our society than good. You have to learn to give back. I don't see you running any charities or having your name put through Orlando in a good way, so the least you can do is give a dollar to someone in need."

"I bought a few kids on the block some backpacks a few years ago, but I thought people would think of me as a hypocrite, so I never did it again.

"Why do you care what other people think of you? If buying backpacks is your way of giving back, then you do that. There is never anything wrong with staying true to who you are and what you believe in. The worst thing you can do to yourself is live a life that you think others think you should be living. Do you and never apologize for being real," she said. "Anyway, I'm starving, so we're going to run into this iHop for a quick bite before we get back on the road. I hope you brought your wallet because I can eat."

"I don't mind buying you something to eat, but I didn't even invite you out. Why do I have to pick up the tab," K.Y asked with sincere curiosity.

"You have the opportunity to run around with a real hustler and learn things that they don't teach you in books. Do you think knowledge is free? Anyway, if you want, I can keep it strictly business like I do with everyone else. I can give you an alias to call me by, see you once a month, so you never forget who the boss is, and never let you get this close to me ever again. From the way you asked about me, I was positive you wanted more than to just see how I move. If I was wrong, let me know so I can take you back to your car and apologize for wasting any of your time tonight. If I'm right, then you're going to do what any man who takes me out does. You're going to pick up the tab."

"Just when I thought we had gotten past the bossy stage, you proved that I was absolutely wrong. I'll pick up the fucking tab."

"Uh-uh-uh. Please don't act like you're doing me any favors. I'll never make you do anything that's not already in your heart to do."

"I want to take you out to get something to eat," he replied.

"Good. Oh, by the way, I never get past the bossy stage. Once you understand that, then you'll understand me a little more."

The girl wasn't lying. K.Y had never watched a female put down so much food in such a short amount of time. He liked that she was clearly able to hold her own in just about everything that she did. Not to mention, she knew how to have a good conversation. They talked about everything from music to politics and what types of books she was reading. She even let her guard down long enough to tell him what bank she worked at on West Colonial Dr. in Orlando. And that she was currently in school at the University of Central Florida for a business degree. She really seemed to have every aspect of her life completely together. He paid for the meal and, at her request, left a generous tip for the young waitress.

"Why do you work a legit job when you make so much doing what you already do," K.Y asked once they were both settled into the car again."

"Uncle Sam is a cruel bastard and just wants his cut off of what I'm making. As you can see, I don't live lavishly because I need to keep him off of my ass. I only put things in my name that my job can pay each month, and I keep the rest of my money in an offshore account somewhere else.

My old man is quite the asshole, but the man has taught me a lot about being smart in my business moves," she said. "Meanwhile, you have a brand new car that has flashy rims, you have flashy clothes, and I would say it's safe to assume you probably live on those same streets that you hustle on."

His silence confirmed to her that everything she was saying is true. "You should be counting your blessings that the pigs haven't raided your spot yet. You're like a big-ass target to them.

How can you afford the things you have, but you can't afford to get out of the hood? Everyone knows you don't shit where you sleep, and the fact that you keep your home so close to your business is beyond dangerous. Anyone who knows you move the amount you do knows exactly where they can run up on you. You need to get your life together," she said bluntly.

"Matter of fact, I knew being around you was bad business for me. I'm just going to drop you back off at your car and make the rest of my rounds before I have to work in the morning. You're young, and you clearly have a lot to learn. I don't know who taught you the game, but they didn't do you much justice."

K.Y. sat there quietly as she belittled his intelligence and his ability to hold his own. He wanted to go off, but he knew he wasn't in a position to. All of his stuff was in his car, so he just wanted to make it back there before he cursed her out like he wanted to.

"It's only a matter of time before you end up screwing yourself if you keep doing business the way you have. I guess I should have known what to expect from a man who comes to make a drop at a studio just a few blocks from a police station with a duffle bag full of drugs, bags, and a scale. You're asking to get caught - or worse.

Something about that last statement pissed him off enough to speak up.

"I've been doing this shit for a full decade before you. Trust, I will be able to operate my business without any of your help or the jewels that you think you're dropping' on me. You're very arrogant, and that same pride will eventually be your downfall," he spat back angrily.

"The bass in your voice is at about a level eight, and I'm going to need you to bring it down to at least a five before I forget I'm trying to be a lady and not curse your ass out.

Don't hold your breath waiting for my downfall because I am arrogant enough to trust the moves I make but wise enough to shut the hell up and listen when someone is trying to school me on some things. I get that I'm only six years older than you, but I've watched real hustlers move and not the petty shit that happens here on these blocks like you've seen."

They were finally in front of Studio 167.

"I'm going to have Beast continue to handle my business deals for me, and when you've had time to calm down and be an adult about the situation, you know how to reach me. Now, get the fuck out."

It took everything in him not to curse her out before slamming her door, but he knew that wouldn't exactly be wise of him. Since Jason stopped selling, Tammy had become his best-selling customer. Even though he threw her a mean discount, he still made money with her, so it didn't make sense to cut their business relationship short.

Because he wasn't in the mood to hear Jason clown him for his high confidence but low performance with the woman he was so buoyant that he could have, he wanted to just get to his care and leave. Just as luck would have it, Jason was walking back into his studio when he saw him scurrying into his car.

"That must have been some date, Casanova," Jason joked. You were gone less than two hours, you got all dressed up, and you didn't even get a good night kiss."

Jason bent over in laughter.

"I'm not in the mood, Jay. That chick has fucking problems, yo. I can see why her bitter ass has been single for so long. Who actually has the time and patience to keep up with someone like that," K.Y. said, clearly frustrated.

"Tee is a challenge because she knows she is worth the fight." He said as he wiped away the tears coming from his eyes. At least one of them was finding serious humor about the situation because K.Y. was pissed.

"You don't find women like that every day, and she knows it. When the man comes along that is going to deal with her crap and put up with all of her shit is how she'll know she found a man that's worth it for her. If you're that determined to get with a woman like that, you have to be willing to see it through all the way," Jason said. "Anyway, my nigga, I tried to warn you before you put yourself out there, but you didn't want to listen. Now that you've had a chance to see how she moves, all of these broads are going to seem lame to you. It's up to you to make a choice if you want to settle with some bird or put up the fight and have a real woman.

Niggas don't get to ride around with her like that. Especially when she's making moves, so what you gonna do? Are you going to make it this far only to say that you made it this far? Or are you going to do what I told you that you needed to do from the very beginning and just stay in your lane?"

***

It had been two weeks since he saw Tammy, and it was clear to K.Y. that she was stubborn and was not going to budge.

He tried going on a few dates, but just like Jason had said, every chick he entertained was lame and not close to worth his time. Even if he hated to admit it, he liked that feisty and independent attitude she possessed.

It was a Monday morning when he decided to stroll into the bank that she worked to take her some flowers and try to make amends with what had happened. When she initially told him that she worked at a bank, he expected her to just be a teller, so he was shocked to see her sitting behind her own desk in her office in the corner. He signaled to the woman at the greeter's desk who he was there to see, and she politely told him to hold. Not even two minutes later, Tammy strutted his way, looking as sexy as ever in her black form-fitting dress and blazer.

"Good morning Mr. Cole," she greeted him warmly. "I hate that you caught me on such a busy morning, but I'll have to reschedule our business meeting for another time. Will you be available today around 3:00 PM," she asked with a beautiful smile on her face.

"Yeah I'll be free," he said, extending the flowers he was holding.

She took a moment to sniff and admire the large bouquet he had just given her. "Thank you. They are gorgeous, but I assure you that you didn't have to do this. I go above and beyond to assist all of my business customers, and I will do whatever it takes to help you. Why don't you meet me at the last establishment that we ate at around 3:00 PM, where we will be able to go into your business needs in more detail, she said.

"Aight bet. I'll be there," he said, barely able to hold back his smile. K.Y was surprised to see her act so warm and inviting to him. He wasn't sure what to expect, but he didn't expect her to be like this. He couldn't wait to see what would transpire later that afternoon.

***

K.Y arrived at the same iHop that they ate at just a few weeks prior, 10 minutes before they were scheduled to meet. He asked the young waitress at the door to seat him at the same table they ate at the last time.

For the first time since he had started dating, K.Y. was actually nervous. For years, he had only cared about money, drugs, and the shit was he was buying. He never cared about women or any serious position that they could play in his life. He only entertained hoes long enough to fuck, and that was in the moment when he could take his attention off of money long enough to do it.

He had always thanked God for his wisdom on not sweating women. He had seen many men lose everything they had ever built after pursuing the wrong woman. He anxiously waited for her arrival. After waiting for twenty minutes, he saw a blocked number calling his phone. He usually wouldn't have answered, but he figured it could have been her since his date was late.

"If you show up at any of my spots uninvited or unannounced again, I will kill you myself," she said with much anger and venom before releasing the line.

CHAPTER TWO

Tammy hated to be so nasty with K.Y., but she knew it was the only way he would understand. It was bad enough doing business with a young man who was so sloppy with his work. Still, she couldn't afford to have any of her enterprises screwed up because of his negligence.

When he walked into the bank, Tammy instantly became enraged. She tried to play it off like she didn't see him, but she noticed him way before he had a chance to speak to Nicole, the bank's greeter.

It was apparent he didn't hear a thing she said about his appearance because he strutted into her job wearing a white tee and pants that were clearly too big. Shit, he didn't even have the decency to have his pants at his waist to hide his drawers.

Usually, Tammy had a thing for dread heads, but his were untidy and uneven. It looked as if he had not seen a touch-up in years. When she first met Kyle, she realized instantly that the young man had a lot of potential if he dealt with the right woman and was willing to learn. So far, he had only shown that he was hot-tempered and disobedient, and she didn't have time to deal with either quality.

Immediately after their first meeting, Jason called her to let her know just how much the young man was feeling her. "My young boy is really feeling your style. I've never seen him so open with someone before. It was like an animal in heat," he joked.

Tamia Santiago was confident but not as arrogant as Kyle had made her seem. Most men were instantly drawn to a woman who didn't vocalize their insecurities. Since Tammy didn't have any, it was no surprise that men seemed to immediately fall in love with her.

The next call she made was to Jason, one of the few people she felt she could actually trust on this earth.

"Beast! What's new?"

"It's the same shit, just a different day, princess. What's going on with you?"

"Your boy walked into the bank like he was invited here. You wouldn't have had anything to do with that, would you?"

"The only thing that I set up was the little meeting you guys had a couple weeks ago. I don't know why you made the mistake of telling that man where you worked anyway. Keep slipping off with your tongue. He will find out where you live before the end of the week," Jason replied, obviously agitated with her sloppiness.

"I know. I know. I got a little carried away in conversation. Kyle let me in with some information, so I figured I could share some stuff so he would feel better about trusting me.."

"Well, don't let it happen again. I promised your old man I would keep an eye out and take good care of you. If you fuck this up, he will have my head. Are we clear on that?"

Tammy didn't doubt a single thing he said. She knew exactly how he was and that he would keep his promise of killing Jason Thompson if anything happened to his princess. "We are crystal clear. I wasn't thinking straight for a moment and put my guard down. I promise it won't happen again."

"Good! I can't afford to be looking over my shoulder when I'm trying to get out of the game. This is my last mission, and I'm out forever."

"I know! You've already preached about how important it is for you to retire. Once I'm comfortable out here, you are free to relax. I won't make any more mistakes."

"You know he really worries about you. He knows you're tough, but he's not sure you can handle something like this."

"Please don't remind me. I've already made up my mind, and I'm going through with this. I need to learn how to do things on my own. He's getting older, and he's not going to be around forever. I'm reminded of that every chance he gets.

When you talk to the old guy, can you tell him that I love him?"

"I got you. Just be careful and watch that fly ass tongue of yours," Jason slid in before hanging up.

Tammy went back to work to finish the rest of the day's tasks. She decided to wait another hour to let K.Y. sweat out her next move before she finally called him back.

"I normally don't answer blocked numbers, so spit it out before I end this damn call," K.Y answered angrily.

"I don't mean to be so abrasive, Kyle. I was just always taught to handle business with an iron fist."

"What was the point in having me drive all the way out there if you knew you weren't gonna show up?"

"I didn't know I wasn't going to have the time to drive up there," she lied. "I got tied up, and anyway, it's probably best that it was handled over the phone. I know for a fact you would have gotten more than the few words I gave you earlier today."

"Whatever, yo. Dis attitude of yours is wild as fuck, and I don't know how much more of it I can take."

"Well, I always told you that you have the choice to stop dealing with me whenever you chose to. If that's what you want to do, then please let me know now so I can call Beast and tell him to cancel the last order I just made."

K.Y. hated that it always seemed like she had the upper hand. No one could get rid of the weight like she was doing, and as much as he wanted to stop dealing with her, he just couldn't afford to do it.

"We can continue to deal with each other business-wise, but I just know now that I can't deal with you on a personal level like I want to."

"That's a shame," she replied. "I was actually curious to see how determined you were. I never thought you would have been such a quitter, but I guess it's best this way. I don't have time for young men who don't know what they want, and clearly, that's what you are.

Beast will continue to handle my transactions, and I'll just deal with you from afar."

"If that's how you want it," he replied.

"To be honest, it's not how I feel, but it's how you feel. I'll respect your wishes and keep everything strictly platonic, and I'll keep my advice and information to myself."

"I never said that I didn't want to deal with you on a more personal level, but it just seems like it's impossible to get what I want with you."

"Do you expect me to read minds? You never clearly told me what you wanted from me."

"I want you to lose the attitude and let me take you out on a real date or something."

"That sounds really nice, but I can hardly afford to do business with someone as hard-headed and sloppy as you are. I don't think I could afford to have a partner like that too."

"You're just so quick to talk shit about me when you've never really given me the chance to see what I was all about," he responded.

"I'm going to text you an address. Be there at 8:00 PM on the dot. Not a minute earlier and not a minute later. If you can't handle those instructions, then don't bother coming at all," just as she had done before, she hung up the line leaving him to wonder what to make of her.

***

Jason sat quietly in the studio to ponder on everything that was going on. *What has this girl gotten me into? I said I was done with this street life already. I can't afford to fuck up and get caught slippin'.*

Jason's family was originally from Jamaica but moved to the states to find and live the 'American Dream.' To his family's surprise, attaining that dream without much family to rely on or any resources to pull from was going to be incredibly difficult. Like most young men who grew up in New York projects, Jason Thompson realized the only way to survive was to find a hustle. He was only 14 years old when he made his first run, and he quickly realized that being the boss is where anyone made the most money.

Delino Santiago was a young hustler who had also just moved to the states. His reign went from his home country of Honduras to Jamaica, the Cayman Islands. He was anxious to extend his business ventures through the east coast of the United States.

"Yo Lino, I'm tired of just doing all of these runs. I want to do something more," young Jason asked the then 30-year-old kingpin.

In his thick accent, he replied, "Show me what else you're capable of, and then we can talk. Oh, and don't you bring any heat to my organization because then I'll have to take care of it the only way I know how to." Delino flashed him his signature grin, yet Jason knew not to mistake it as an act of being friendly.

The young boy took a long time to ponder what he could do before getting the idea from his long-time best friend, Patrick Bennett.

"The fastest way to make money is to do it from product that we don't have to pay for. A couple of guys on the Avenue are trying to move in on Lino's territory. Let's grab their product and make it impossible for them to make money on these blocks. We'll put a couple dollars in our pocket, and we'll be acting as security for Lino. Are you in or what?"

Without hesitation, Jason replied, "What are we waiting on?"

That evening, the men waited until the young hustlers on the block came back with fresh product from their trap houses a few blocks down.

Patrick and Jason were only 14, but they were built like grown men. Jason was already 6'1, and Patrick was only an inch shorter than he was. Although neither of them had their permits to drive, Patrick drove his grandmother's beat-up Buick down the Avenue to rob the young boys.

"What you need, son," the unsuspecting victim asked Jason when the vehicle slowed down in front of him.

"That depends on what you got. I need some good shit, and I wanna see the product before I buy anything."

"Then get yo' ass out the car and come check this shit out," the young man replied.

"I would, but I just got in an accident a few weeks ago. Sadly, I can't walk anymore. My man right here don't know product like I do, so I can't trust him to look it over for me," he lied. "I got the money, and you got the product, so are you trying to make this money or just chat with me on this block?"

The young hustler walked over to the vehicle and discreetly stuck his hand inside to show the men his product. Without much effort, Jason pulled the young man into the car and stuck him down between his legs.

Patrick knew they were going to rob him but never imagined it going down like this.

"What the fuck you staring at, man? Get us the fuck outta here," Jason screamed out to his friend.

"Just take whatever you want and let me go," the young boy pleaded from his cramped space.

Jason used his right arm to punch the boy square in the face, and it was instantly lights out for him. He emptied out the man's pockets for all of his drugs and money with lightning speed and threw the bag he was carrying that had his heat and more product in the back seat.

"Slow down over here where there isn't much light so I can get this bum outta the car."

Patrick did just as he was told, and he watched his friend open the door and maneuver the man out of the vehicle.

"What the fuck? You're a beast nigga! I swear I've never seen or heard of any shit like that. How the hell did you manage to fit his big ass in that little ass space with you still sitting in the passenger seat? You didn't have room to cock your arm back much, but you had enough power in your hit to knock him out immediately!"

From that day on, Patrick and everyone on the streets referred to Jason as Beast. He built a reputation that he would hit first and ask questions later, and with a punch like his, no one ever wanted to find out first hand. Delino was obviously impressed at the young man's work and gave him the chance to work security for him and his family.

"I'm going out of town, and I need you to handle something super important to me," Delino spoke in his heavy accent. "My wife and I haven't had a vacation since she had the baby, so we are getting out of the country. I don't want to hear a single thing about you being on these streets because I need you at my house, keeping an eye out 24/7. If you do this job right, I promise you can make enough to go into early retirement."

"I got you, Lino."

Beast had been trying to set a meeting up with Lino and Patrick for months, but Patrick didn't want any part of it.

"I don't work for anyone but myself! I don't take orders from anyone because I am my own fucking boss," Patrick replied when Beast tried to see if he had any interest in a job like his.

"I'm telling you, man. I'm about to make some real fucking money. Why wouldn't you want to be a part of something like this?"

"Do you not understand English? Mi bad from mi born! I don't need another man to make any money when I'm smart and bad enough to do it alone. I'm a stick-up kid; I always have been, and I probably always will be."

"Nigga, when you get tired of robbing these corner stores and hustlers, then you let me know. It doesn't make sense to put yourself at such a risk when you can make some good money doing absolutely nothing at all."

Jason really wanted to help his boy out, but he knew he would be beating a dead horse if he continued to press the issue. After Jason's first successful mission as acting as a security guard for Lino's little girl, it became his only job.

Lino was very active on the blocks and always made it appear to those on them that he had no other life besides being a hustler. He never let anyone know just how much of a family man he really was. Jason's security job often required him to travel and be gone for really long periods. Still, the money he received was well worth it. Whenever he was in town, he always linked up with his best friend Patrick, and they would do what he did best to make some fast cash.

"You like to play this uppity shit since you high rollin' with a semi-legit job, but you and I both know you're still a stickup kid like me. Some things never change no matter how much we want them to," Patrick told him after they hit their biggest lick ever.

Jason never liked referring to himself like that, but he knew what his friend had told him was true. Jason wanted nice things and blowing some of the best trees. Whenever they robbed a hustler, he could always get some nice jewelry, sneakers, and green without having to spend any money. It just made it even better that he was able to put more money in his pockets when the jobs were done.

Now, Jason was firm on his decision to go completely legit, and the transition had been hard for him because all he really knew was a life of crime. He had been caught and served minor time in county jail for some of his actions, but he was tired of putting himself in jeopardy to live any more of his precious life behind bars.

I stopped buying weight a minute ago, Jason thought to himself. *I said I was done and a hundred percent legit. I don't know how I let Tee and her old man drag me into this shit again.*

***

"I'm glad to see you can finally follow some directions," Tammy said after Kyle pulled up at the address she gave him at exactly 8:00 PM.

"You can cut the funny shit, shawty. I don't take orders from anyone, so this whole thing is new to me anyway."

"Get used to it. I've always been in charge, and I always will be. You're cute, but that isn't going to keep me interested forever. Park and leave your heat in the car. We'll be taking my vehicle tonight."

K.Y. really didn't want to leave his protection in his car again, but he figured since nothing popped off the last time he rolled with her that it should be ok to do it again. He did as he was told and climbed into the passenger side of her car.

"So is this where you live," he asked her. "This area is really nice and expensive out here."

CHARGE IT TO THE GAME

"I'm sure you would like to know where I rest my head, but that's for me to know and for you to find out only if you play your cards right," she responded.

"Before you go anywhere with me, we have to get your look together. I'm stopping by my good friend's salon; you really need to cut off that shit that's on your head. You would look so much better with a low cut anyway."

"You're bossy with your business deals, and you even try to boss around the men that you date," he stated, clearly annoyed.

"You said I never gave you a serious chance, and I'm doing it now. Guys that I have dated in the past have been up to my standards, and if you don't want to be, we can just remain business partners. You have such a cute face, and that messed up mop on the top of your head really does just takes away from it."

K.Y didn't respond and just stared straight ahead.

"I know I'm a lot to deal with, but I'm sure you deal with me because you know, in the end, it will all pay off. No matter what happens, I always leave something better than when I find it. Trust me.

I don't know if Jason told you, but I'm usually a loner. I don't date many guys, and I just stay to myself. My father left some pretty big shoes to fill, so I always hold everyone I deal with to a very high standard. I've seen it all done before, so I know that what I'm asking for is not much. I'm prepared to stay alone as long as I have to until I'm sure I've found exactly what it is that I'm looking for."

"I feel you shawty, but you also have to learn to step back and not be in control all of the time. If your father handled his business with an iron fist, then I'm sure he wasn't used to taking orders from anyone. If that's the case, then why wouldn't you take a step back and let a man be a man for a change?"

"I'm willing to take a step back and play that submissive woman role if the right man does ever come along. In case you can't tell, I'm a businesswoman. I'm about my money, my education, and my businesses.

I don't have much time to entertain men. I like to make sure I get the weak ones out early. Despite that you follow my orders, I don't believe you're weak. I recognize that it takes a bigger man to be able to shut up when he would really prefer to cuss me out instead," she chuckled. "When I've found the perfect guy, I will know it, but in the meantime, I'm just going to work my ass off and do me."

Tammy pulled up in front of the hair salon where she usually got her hair done and put the vehicle in park.

"I didn't think that hair salons actually stayed open this late," he stated.

"Normally, they don't, but I asked my girl here to stay and hook you up. She's already been paid for this job, so if you don't go in there, then I would have just wasted some of my money on you," she said.

"Look at it this way, even if you and I don't end up the way you want to, wouldn't you like me to help you get your business to another level? You're never going to get there as long as you allow yourself to look like the rest of these dope boys out here. You wear your clothes too big, and your hair is always messy. It's time for people to see Kyle Cole, the businessman, instead of just K.Y the neighborhood dope boy."

What she was saying made a lot of sense. K.Y had been the victim of racial profiling many times before and hated it. He always figured it was wiser to just blend in with the crowd instead of trying to stand out. He never really considered doing anything that would make him much different than his competitors on the block.

"Anyway, unless you're on a spiritual journey, it's just hair. If you don't like it, then you can always grow it back out and just make sure it stays nice and neat," Tammy said as she was getting out of the vehicle.

"Now remember, this is a hair salon, and women love to talk. You and I are just friends. Only if they ask you, I'm helping you start a business venture. That is it," she demanded firmly. "I don't like it when a lot of people know my business."

To Tammy's surprise, K.Y went in the salon and handled himself a lot better than she would have ever expected. None of the ladies in the salon seemed to know who he was or what his preferred occupation choice was, which she liked because she had a reputation that she needed to protect.

"I'm actually kind of glad you forced me to do this," K.Y said. "I was getting tired of those locks on my head, and this does look better on me," K.Y said happily as they were getting back in the car. "I've thought about it for a while, but I never made the decision to finally go through with it. It's just been a part of my looks for years."

"I knew it would, and I'm glad you like it too. We are getting ready to take your business to the next level, and your look needs to change with it. In addition to changing your look, we have to switch up the way you carry yourself and the reputation that you currently have in these streets.

We're going to make one more stop to get you out of those terrible clothes, and then we can move on to the fun stuff."

"I don't pass judgment on you or your clothes, so why do you always gotta go there with me," he huffed.

"First of all, I keep my shit tight so that no one will ever be able to pass judgment on what I wear or how I carry myself. Most importantly, I do it because you're so bright, but you clearly don't know how to use it.

You don't think other people pass judgment on you when you open your mouth and speak the way you do, or because you prefer to wear expensive clothes that are way too big for you?

You have no income on paper to the feds, yet you can afford to have the nice things you do. Do you really think that people are that stupid?

Luckily for you, you seem like you have enough common sense to not let other people around you know that you are moving as much as you are. Because if you did, you would have been under the jail a long time ago," she said. "I get that you want to live a life of luxury, and you work hard enough that you should be able to, but it is all in how you do it."

Please don't take this the wrong way, but I was shocked to hear you speak to those ladies in the salon the way you did. I don't know if it's your thick country accent or if it is your usual choice of words, but you typically sound kind of unintelligent to me. It's time that you switch up your look and how you speak.

You have to keep people on their toes because you never want to be considered predictable. If that happens, it will be too easy for someone to catch you slipping."

"You're really rude, bossy, arrogant, and you think you have the answers to everything. You don't know it all in case no one ever told you that," K.Y responded to her statement.

"I'm not rude; I'm just bluntly honest. You're right about me being bossy and arrogant, but it hasn't failed me in almost three decades, so I'm clearly doing something right.

A wise man knows that he knows nothing at all, so I have to disagree with you there. I don't know it all. That's why I have learned to shut the hell up when someone with a little more experience or knowledge is speaking to me about something that I can use or something that could benefit me one day. There is a difference between simply hearing someone and actually actively listening to someone. You really should learn it because you might be surprised where it could potentially take you one day."

"Well you could have fooled me in the way you act towards me. You seem to think that you have all the answers to all of my problems and how I live," K.Y. spat back.

"My old man taught me years ago that a smart man learns from his mistakes, and a wise man learns from the mistakes of others. I have watched many people live great in this game, and I have seen many more fail miserably, all for the love of the same game. Please notice that I never said I have watched someone be successful in this game," she paused for a few seconds before she began speaking again. "Excuse me for sounding a little sentimental, but I just don't want to see that happen to you. Something about you makes me want to help you and teach you some of the things that I have seen that have worked for others."

K.Y was a little thrown off by her last statement because it was the first time that she had ever really shown him any type of affection or genuine concern.

"Is that emotion you're showing," he joked. "It looks good on you. You should wear it more often."

"Shut up," Tammy replied as she jokingly slapped his shoulder.

"Don't get used to it, and you better keep this between you and me. I can't have niggas out here thinking that Tamia Santiago is out here going soft."

They both laughed.

"I guess I never looked at it that way, but now that you've made yourself clear - I'm all ears. I'm ready to learn whatever you have to teach me," K.Y. said.

"Good."

CHAPTER THREE

"Damn young blood! I almost didn't recognize you when I first saw you," Jason said as he took off his headphones and took a break from making a beat.

"I've been hanging out with Tammy lately. She has made a few suggestions that I have been open to listening to," K.Y responded as he took a seat on the comfortable sofa in Jason's studio. "I'm trying to look like a businessman instead of just some dope dealer."

Instead of his standard baggy attire, K.Y was wearing a nice three-piece suit with some leather loafers. "That definitely sounds like something she would say," Jason chuckled. "I hate to sound so surprised, but I have to admit that I am quite surprised that the two of you have been spending much time together. What's going on with you two?"

"We're just chilling and getting to know each other, I guess. A month ago I cut all of my hair off and went shopping for some new clothes. We went out to dinner a few times, and she's actually let me come to the bank where she works, so this business I'm starting looks legit. She wants other business people to see me as a businessman. She wants the reputation that I have around here to change a little."

"I'm glad to hear that. Tammy's been around for quite a while, so she knows a lot about the street life. Her father was a real successful man back in the day, so she knows a lot more than most."

"What do you mean he *was* successful," K.Y asked his friend. Although him and Tammy had been spending a lot of time together, they rarely talked about their families. They would both briefly bring it up, but neither would go into detail and the other one would never force it.

"You know everyone has their time, and he had his. His reign went on for decades, but it was time for him to rest. Don't get it twisted, though; Mr. Santiago was always smart about his business moves, so that man will be rich forever," Jason stated. "Anyway, what brings you down here to see me?"

"I've been making a few changes to how I spend my money, and I was interested in finding out if you need an investor for this place. I need a few legit spots to throw some money around, and what better place than my own homeboy's spot."

"Youngin, that sounds very wise of you, and that lets me know that you are clearly listening and taking notes when Tee is speaking to you. I just don't think it's a good idea. I've lost close friendships over faulty business deals, and I'm not trying to go there with you. We've been rocking for far too long for a few dollars to come in between that. Ya feel me?

If you're serious about making some good investments, then I can set up a few business deals for you. All I need you to do is to remain my boy and look out for that little brat," Jason said. "I love that little one to death, but I really will end up seeing an early grave if anything happens to her.

If I didn't trust you the way that I do, you can believe that I would never let you two out of my sight, but I think you're a good stand-up dude, and I think that could be something Tee could use."

"I appreciate that, and I agree with you. I think that she needs someone like me, but it sometimes seems like she doesn't always agree with it."

Jason replied, "I don't think that's it. This whole thing is new for her. Tee normally does her own thing, and those who she deals with don't have the balls to handle someone as headstrong as she is. They typically bounce early. That's why I warned you in the beginning about what you would be getting yourself into. That's enough with the love shit, man. I'm not use to talking to you about this kind of stuff," Jason laughed. "I got an artist coming through in a minute, and he is really looking for a solid investor. I'll make sure I let him know that I have one that might be interested. Why don't you hang around for a few minutes so you can meet him yourself," Jason suggested.

The two men sat around smoking and goofing off until a large man walked through the door with an entourage 10 deep. His stature made it impossible to miss him, and his rugged appearance demanded everyone's attention.

"Scheme, what's up, my man," Jason greeted his artist. "I hope you ready to lay down this fire so we can finally get you out on these streets, on these radio stations, and in these clubs."

"Come on, Jay," the man replied in his deep voice. "You know I'm always ready to put something down with these hot beats you got. I swear no one in Florida can come close to the beats and songs you've produced for me. I hope you don't mind that I brought more heads than expected, but a few of my boys came to visit and wanted to see me put in work."

"Nah, it's never an issue. Don't let me find out one of these niggas got some talent and needs to be in this booth with you," Jason said hopefully.

Jason was definitely a businessman and was always looking for a way to expand. "As a matter of fact, I got my mans here that I wanted to introduce you to. His name is K.Y, and he's an investor looking to put a few of his dollars in a wise place. I told him that you and I think ya'll should link up."

K.Y nodded his head in his direction as his way of saying hi. Scheme returned the gesture.

"I've got a few moves that I'm trying to make, and I really can use someone who has a few dollars to back me up. Why don't you leave me with your business card, and I will make sure to have someone from my camp contact you later this week," Scheme suggested.

"I just ordered some new business cards, and I haven't received them in the mail yet," K.Y. lied while making a mental note to order some. "I've already got my number written out here. Hit me up," K.Y. said as he handed him a sheet of paper with his name and information on it.

"Bet."

***

"I hope you have a good reason as to why you are late to the business dinner that you suggested," Tammy snapped as Kyle took his seat.

"I know you're mad, but I do have a good reason. I finally took your advice to move some money into a legit business, and I had to meet up with the dude," K.Y. said while he was taking a look at his menu.

Tammy and Kyle had practically been inseparable for the last four weeks. They frequently spoke on the phone or through e-mails, and they made it a habit to try a new restaurant together at least three times a week. Tonight, they were trying out a unique establishment that one of Tammy's friends had strongly recommended.

Ned's Restaurant had received raving reviews, and they had to try out the hottest soul and seafood spot.

"Well, it's about time you got off of your ass and did something on your own. I'm proud of you."

"Of course, you had to say something smart because just giving me the compliment would have been too hard for you to do."

"And here I thought you didn't know me, and it's obvious that you do," she replied with a sly grin. "So what information did you get about this potential business opportunity."

"Well, I didn't want to be too late, so I just gave the guy my information, and he said he would be in touch."

"You mean to tell me that you showed up late but didn't accomplish anything. Did you even get the person's name or their contact information?"

"He is one of Jason's artists, and his name is Scheme. I didn't get his information, but I did manage to give him my number and e-mail."

"You don't even have decent business cards to hand out. I'm sure you did something unprofessional like write it down on a small piece of paper that is liable to be lost or not thought about later," she said without removing her eyes from her menu.

K.Y.'s silence was all that she needed to prove that she also knew him a lot better than he thought.

"Did you at least make that drop before you got here? You know I really needed to get that product to one of my clients, and I wasn't going to have the time to do it myself."

"I was already running late, and I didn't want to piss you off by coming later. I called your client and told her that I would be dropping it off later this evening."

"Just when I thought you were learning something from me, you once again proved that you're hardheaded and will do whatever you feel like doing. You showed up late to handle 'your business'. Still, nothing was accomplished, so now that means my business didn't get handled either," Tammy threw her menu down on the table. "I have to run to the restroom. I need you to get on the phone and get this person's contact information now so we can start making moves. When I get back, you at least have a number and some sort of knowledge on this business opportunity that made you late and unable to handle my business." Tammy stormed off.

As much as he hated how little she would make him feel, he knew that what she was saying was right. He disliked feeling like he was taking orders from her, but he realized it had to be done. He waited a few minutes before calling Jason on his cell phone.

"What's up youngin. I'm working. What do you need," Jason yelled over the loud music in the background.

"I wanted to know if you could get me Scheme's information so that I can call him later. Did you know exactly what he needed money to fund anyway," K.Y. asked.

Jason took a minute to respond, and it was apparent that he was trying to move to a quieter location. "I'll text you his number as soon as we get off of the phone, but I know he said something about starting his own management and PR Company. Right now, he is under my label, but he came up with the idea to expand. Usually, I wouldn't want my artist to do his own thing like this, but he knows some big names in high places. He said he is determined to do it on his own without his connects though. He wants them to see what he is capable of, so they drop some big money when they invest. It will be a good look to get on board with something like that while the numbers are still low, ya feel me?

Anyway, I need to get back to work, so I'll send you that text and get up with you later," without waiting for K.Y.'s response, Jason disconnected the line.

Just as he finished up his phone call, Tammy came back and took her seat at the table. "Well," she started. "Did you do what I told you to do?"

"Can you cut it out and stop talking to me like that? I did exactly what you suggested for me to do."

"I will not cut it out or take it easier on you until you become smarter in the moves that you make. I realize that I can be challenging, but until you learn how to think for yourself, I will continue to treat you like this," Tammy snapped back.

"Jason just text me the man's number. He said that he is starting his own management company. He also said that he is confident that this can blow up."

"If Jason thinks it's a money-making machine, it probably is. Send me the information and I will take care of everything from here. As much as I want to trust you to get this done on your own, your track record shows me that it will not get done properly unless I take care of it myself."

K.Y. returned to looking at his menu to keep from telling her what he really wanted to say.

"I will deal with him as if I am your secretary, and you just have to make sure that if I ever come up in discussion, you keep the charade going," she said.

"I can do that," K.Y. responded. "While we are on the topic of titles, what exactly are we," he asked.

"I guess I'm not really sure how to respond to that silly question you just asked me." Tammy responded as she picked up the menu to avoid the awkward conversation he had just started.

"Shit, you and I spend a large amount of time together, which leads me to believe that we are somewhat exclusive, but you have never acknowledged me as your man."

"Kyle, please don't go there with me. I have expressed to you that when I am ready to settle down, I will. I have not yet reached that point. Unfortunately, I haven't found someone worthy of being able to call me their woman. Every time I think you might be the one to get me to do it, you will do something like you did today that proves to me that you are not quite ready. You really should be worrying about building your business properly before trying to claim a woman in the first place," she said. "Contrary to what you believe, you are not the only man who is trying to prove themselves to me."

K.Y. didn't know how to respond to her statement, so he decided to leave it alone. The waitress came to their table, and the two of them placed their orders. While the attractive waitress was taking their order, she never once looked in Tammy's direction. Instead, she stayed focused and engaged only with K.Y.

"I think that waitress has a thing for you," Tammy giggled after the waitress walked away. "Do you want me to get her number for you?"

"Don't front like you're not jealous," K.Y. stated, hoping that it was true.

"Ha! Please don't flatter yourself. The beautiful thing about being confident is that another attractive woman doesn't intimidate me. I know what I can offer to the right person. If you would rather settle for something like that than to work to proving yourself to a real woman, then that means that I already won by narrowing down my options."

"Whatever! You can pretend like you don't care, but the fact that you have been spending so much time either with me or talking to me leads me to believe that you don't exactly mean what you say."

"You are free to interpret my actions however you want to, but I've already let you know what the deal is. I don't care what you think about this situation as long as you make sure anyone who knows you knows that I'm strictly a friend, and you handle my business."

K.Y. chose to drop the conversation.

The two spent the rest of the dinner conversing about music and the last few movies they had checked out. Even though the evening started rough, the rest of the night went by smoothly.

"I'm going to grab my car from the valet, and then I'll meet you by your vehicle, so I can finish this run myself," Tammy stated as she stood up.

"How did you know that I didn't give my car to the valet," K.Y. asked.

"I have enough faith to know that you are smart enough not to hand over keys to your car with pounds of product in it, and I also had to pick up your keys from the table, or you would have forgotten them. Where would you be without me?"

"That's a good question and one that I never want to be answered," he said while he took his keys back from her while admiring her beauty lovingly.

Kyle walked over to the car and waited for Tammy as they had discussed.

"Let's make this quick. I've already had this woman waiting for hours," Tammy stated as she backed into the parking space next to his.

K.Y. popped his trunk and instantly knew something wasn't right. He moved some items around and then began to panic when he realized that what he was looking for was no longer in the spot that he left it in.

"It's not here," he said, barely audible.

"How could it not be there? Didn't you pick it up earlier?"

"Of course, I picked it up, but I know I left it here, and now it's not here," he said while raising his voice.

"What the hell am I supposed to do now? I already paid you for my product. Now, you're trying to use the oldest trick in the book by claiming to have gotten robbed."

"I'm not trying to play anything, so cut it out! I picked it up, went to the studio, and then came here. I never once moved it, and I know exactly where I placed it."

"So then I guess my shit just grew legs and walked off then, huh? If you had done this shit when I told you to handle it, there would not have even been a reason to have this fucking conversation."

"Watch who the fuck you're talking to because I'm not in the mood for this shit right now," K.Y snapped as his voice became louder. A couple walking to their vehicle even stopped to look at the two in their apparent disagreement.

"You better watch your tone and who the hell you're speaking to," Tammy said in a stern whisper. "Now I'm out of money, and I have to get this stuff to my largest client for her party tonight. Just because you screw up does not mean that I will be doing the same also. I don't care what you have to do, but I want another ten pounds delivered to the address where you picked me up a month ago. I want it done in the next thirty minutes, and I need it understood that I will not be paying a dime for your negligence. If you can't handle that, then just know that you made the decision to cut all ties that we have together going forward." With that, Tammy got back into her car and sped off.

CHAPTER FOUR

Tammy waited impatiently at the neighborhood sign that she told Kyle to meet her. He was already five minutes late, and she was beginning to wonder if she had been too hard on him at the restaurant. Just as she was about to walk back to her car and permanently delete his number, she noticed his all-black Dodge Charger speeding into the complex.

"I almost thought you weren't going to show," she stated as she walked over to the driver's side window. "No need to cut the car off. I'm just going to grab my stuff and go."

"I understand you being upset that things were not handled the way you asked me to handle them, but do you honestly think I wanted this to happen? Now, I have to take that huge loss of product," he retorted.

"We are all free to make our own choices, but the consequences will always cost us. I asked you to drop the product off before you came to dinner. If that had been done, you wouldn't be going through this now. When will you learn that I'm not just some miserable, bossy bitch? I act the way I do for a reason. Besides, I already knew you had a few snakes in your camp; I just didn't know that they would have shown themselves so early."

"You haven't met any of my niggas, so how can you assume I hang out with anyone flawed," he asked. "I've been rolling with the same niggas for years, and I don't think any of them would have done me like this."

"Do you think Eve would have eaten fruit from the tree that she was forbidden to eat from if the serpent would have come out and told her his real intentions?" Tammy asked him, then left him with a moment of silence to let him think about it.

"It doesn't matter how long you've been rolling with somebody. What has any of those motherfuckers done for you lately to help take you to the next level?," she continued. "When was the last time any of them did anything selflessly for your benefit? Of course, these bastards are going to smile in your face and act like everything is kosher. You're the reason these fools can put money in their pockets and food on their table.

You honestly don't think anyone in your camp would lie, steal, or kill to be in the position you're in or for a chance to make the kind of money you're making?

You just took this loss tonight, and you're not going to be losing much sleep over it. Can your 'friends' manage that kind of loss and bounce back," she asked. "Of course, they wouldn't be able to.

Only a few people know that you had the product on you and in the trunk of your car. You did, but you wouldn't have any motive to try to hide your own product because you know I don't play with my business or my money. I did, but I was with you tonight, and you know that I handle my business and never allow myself to be put in situations like this.

Thanks to this shit, I have to discount this much more than I want to because I can't afford to lose her as a client. You need to consider who in your camp is there for the greater good and who is sitting, waiting to slit your throat." Tammy leaned into the driver's side window and popped the trunk before she gave him a light peck on the cheek. "You're young, and you still have a lot to learn. Not everyone who smiles in your face is on your team and not everyone you call a friend deserves the actual title.

I'm going to handle this and then lay low for a few days. I need you to use this time wisely. Think with an open mind who is trying to sink your organization. I care about you, but I can't let my team fall just because you have a hard time believing that it's time to cut a few snakes loose. Once I feel like you've had enough time to think this through, I will call you. In the meantime, you need to keep your ears and eyes open, and most importantly, your mind. Be safe, take it easy, and don't do anything stupid or get in any kind of trouble." She walked to the back of his car, grabbed the duffle bags full of product from the trunk, and got back into her Toyota. She looked at him and blew him a little kiss before driving away.

***

Kyle decided to just drive around for a while before heading back to the hood. *Who the hell would steal from me? I'm good to everyone around me, and I make sure everyone who rolls with me eats good.* He thought to himself.

In an effort to narrow his choices, K.Y. went through the events of his day.

Before K.Y went to meet with Jason in the studio, he went to see one of his connects on Mercy Drive. K.Y had been doing business with his boy Dante for years, and they never seemed to have any bad blood between the two of them. Whenever he met with D, he always made sure to keep it strictly professional. He never dared to talk to him about where he laid his head or any of his personal relationships or moves. *Nah, it couldn't have been D because he knows that I normally get rid of my product as fast as I get it. He didn't even know that I was going out to eat tonight, much less where I would be eating at.*

The next stop he made was to Jason's studio, but he didn't even have to give that much thought. *Jason was at the studio working, and I know he wouldn't have done that for shit that belongs to Tammy. I didn't even tell him I had anything on me, so it couldn't have been him.*

Then, he remembered that he ran into Rashard while he was on his way out from Jason's studio.

Rashard and K.Y had been friends since they were just young boys in middle school. He always considered Rashard to be like family because they had been down for each other for so long. When Rashard's mother passed away when they were only 16, Kyle's mom had taken him in and allowed him to live with them. She even raised him like one of her own. K.Y had put Rashard on with him when he started making some real money on the streets.

He would have him make runs for him and even helped him by throwing him a few extra dollars just because he wanted to look out for him.

***

"Big bruh, what's going on? I ain't seen yo' ass in months! What the hell you been up to," Rashard asked in his thick country accent.

"Ain't shit, I just been working. It's the same shit, just a different day."

"I be asking bout you in the hood, and niggas say you hardly on the block anymore. You goin legit or something?" Rashard asked.

41

"You know I love dese streets too much to even joke like that," K.Y responded. "I just been chillin' with this new shawty who helping a nigga try to move up in the world. I guess I been spending more time with her than I spend on the block, that's all."

"Well it looks like you still eating good, bruh. You got on flashy suits and driving around that new car and shit, so whatever shawty got you on must be working."

"Yeah I guess you can say that. Thanks to her help, I even been moving more than I was moving before."

"Damn, and you was already moving a lot before, so that means she really gettin' yo shit together. That's what's up. You too busy with ya boo to be checking for us little niggas anymore," he joked.

"Nah bih, it's not even like that. Her and I are just cool. I'm actually getting ready to go check out this new restaurant with her now. She said that her people's been telling her that new spot Ned's is the shit, so she wanna check it out."

"Yeah, I heard that food is good over there. It's really fancy and shit just to be a nigga joint," Rashard laughed. "So what's up? You don't have any runs that a nigga could be doing right now. It's like you going big time and forgot about the small fish who helped you get there."

"I got some shit on me, but I'm going to try to handle that myself before I leave. I'll hit you up as soon as I have some moves to make that way you can put a few extra dollars in ya pocket, bruh."

***

Why would Rashard, of all people, have a hand in trying to sink me? I'm his baby's Godfather, and I've always been there for him and his family. Whenever Jr. needed anything, I bought it. Shit, I always pay him more than I pay any of my others runners. This nigga betta not have had any part in setting me up because if so, I'll off that fool my damn self before he causes any more issues in my business.

CHAPTER FIVE

K.Y had been going crazy thinking that his own best friend would steal from him, but it didn't help that what Tammy said would only be a few days turned into two weeks.

Every time he tried to reach out to her, the phone would go immediately to voicemail. Her voicemail box filled up within the first 2 days of her being away. He sent her a few e-mails to make sure that she was ok, but after his third e-mail, he received one back saying there was an issue with the e-mail address he was trying to contact. He thought about showing up at her job but realized immediately that it would be a bad idea. Instead, he decided to call the bank and mask his voice to see if he could get any information that way.

"I'm sorry, sir, but Ms. Santiago is on vacation. I can transfer you to her voicemail, and she will get back to you as soon as she returns," Nicole, the bank's greeter, said to him after his third attempt. After he agreed to the transfer, the phone rang a few times before being answered by her voicemail.

"You have reached the voicemail box of Tamia Santiago. I will be out of the office starting September 19th, and I will be returning on October 3rd. Please forward all of your immediate requests to one of my colleagues or leave a detailed message so that I can call you." K.Y didn't let the voicemail finish before he disconnected the call.

Why would she have told me a few days if she knew she was taking a full two weeks off? He thought. He checked the calendar and realized that it was already the 2nd, so he knew he should be hearing something from her soon.

K.Y decided it was in his best interest to lay low for the next few days because he knew that she would have him busier than he had ever been as soon as she got back.

Instead of being on the block or making runs, he took time to just relax and get caught up watching some bootleg movies his boys had given him to check out. A whole week went by, and he still had not heard a single word from Tammy. He was beginning to get really worried until he received a call from a blocked number. "Hello," he answered the phone.

"Yeah, you already know who this is. What's up," the familiar voice he had been waiting to hear asked.

"How the hell do you think you can just bounce for this long and call me back like everything is good," he asked, obviously aggravated.

"Well, hello, friend. It's nice talking to you too. Is that how you greet all of your friends that call you," she asked him.

"No, it's not, and it's because I don't look at you as just my friend. You and I are way better than you just doing the disappearing act the moment that I take a loss," he said. "Where have you been?"

"Shut the hell up, and don't fucking question me. I've had my own shit to deal with, and I didn't call you to hear this crap.

I was going to tell you that I'm going back to Ned's tonight. You can meet me there so we can get caught up, and you can tell me if you've been able to figure anything out about this mystery case we have on our hands.

I'll be there in 30 minutes. You can meet me there or not," Tammy spat before hanging up.

As angry as he was with her disappearing act, he was happy to know that she was at least ok. He got up and quickly got dressed to meet her.

He walked into the restaurant and was thrilled to finally see Tammy's face again. Suddenly, he forgot how mad he was at her because he knew that she would help him figure all this mess out.

"Hey there," she said excitedly as she stood up to give him a hug.

"What's up, stranger? I almost thought you forgot who I was," he joked.

"Cut the crap, Kyle. I had a few things I had to deal with myself, and I had to sit back from afar to see how you handled your first loss."

K.Y. was instantly puzzled by her last statement.

"This isn't my first loss. In case you forgot, I have been in these streets for a while."

"Well, this was your first loss since you've been dealing with me. In my experience, men become overly paranoid and begin to doubt the loyalty of all of those in their circle after a new member comes in and they take a hit. I couldn't take the risk of you trying to retaliate against me or something. Were you ever able to figure out who it could have potentially been?"

"Unfortunately, I did."

"I assume from the somber response that I was right about you having a snake smiling in your face."

"I'm not a hundred percent sure, but it only makes sense to be one person. I never thought you would have set me up because ten pounds is light for you, so you never had to worry about me retaliating on you."

"Good. I'm glad you realize that. I may be a lot of things, but a thief is not one of them. I already placed your order because I didn't want you to be too distracted to let me know what you figured out. So who is it, and why do you think that they did it."

"I just have this feeling that my boy Rashard was the one who pulled this shit off."

"This is my first time hearing his name. Who is he, and why do you think he had something to do with it?"

K.Y. began to explain to Tammy just how close he and Rashard had been through the years and how the death of Rashard's mother brought them closer together.

"My mother even raised him as her own son. It didn't matter that we didn't always have the best of everything, but my mom made sure to share with him whatever we owned. He stuck around when I figured out that my own mother was hooked on some of the shit that I was selling out on these streets," Kyle said with evident disappointment in his voice.

This was the first time K.Y had ever gone into any detail about his mother, and now it made sense to Tammy.

"I'm sorry to hear that," she responded. "Sometimes we like to take the blame for other's habits because we know that we are partly to blame for the product being so easily available on the streets. You have to remember that if she was meant to be an addict, it would have happened no matter your profession. Everything happens for a reason."

"I've tried to tell myself that over and over, but it still doesn't make the situation easier. My mom went from being a sweet, loving, and caring woman to being a monster. She stole and sold her body just to be able to chase a high. She had stolen product from me and had even done some things I would rather not repeat to niggas I knew on the block just for a hit. It's embarrassing and hurtful."

"Where is she now?"

"Somewhere on someone's block chasing a hit. I haven't seen that woman in years, and she knows that she is no longer safe in Pine Hills. She made a lot of enemies out here."

"Have you ever thought of trying to get her some help or going to look for her?"

"I tried putting her into rehab a couple times. The woman just doesn't want the help, and you can't make someone do something that they don't want to do.

I think that's a big part of the reason why I never moved from my home. I wanted her to have a way to contact me in case she ever decided that she wanted to get help. She bought that house when we were babies, and I just never had the heart to give it up."

"Damn. You just made me feel like a jerk for some of my comments about you never moving out of the hood. I can understand why you feel that way, but it's important to think about you and your future too. It sounds to me like you've already accepted that things are the way they are and that nothing is going to change until she does. So why don't you try to piece together your life and move on," she asked. "I have a friend of mine that is looking to rent a small house and isn't picky on the area. Why don't I introduce you two, and if things go smoothly, you can let her rent it. That way, if your mother ever does come back, you will have someone in the house that can pass on the message to you. Staying in that house and doing your business there also is not helping you out."

"I've been thinking a lot about that since this whole thing popped off. Give me a minute to think this all through thoroughly, and then we can talk about you setting up a meeting with her."

"Take all the time you need. After all, that is your mom's house that we are talking about, and I can understand that it's a big part of you. So Rashard grew up in that same house with you?"

"Yeah, he did. We took him in, and when I started making money, I always made sure that nigga ate too. That's why I just have such a hard time believing that he would be capable of doing something like this to me. I was there for that fool when no one else gave two shits about him. Why would he want to steal from me when all I've ever tried to do was help him?"

"It sounds crazy, but sometimes people that you help resent you for the help instead of appreciating you like they should."

"Why the hell would anyone want to bite off the hand that feeds them?"

"I'm assuming that you and Rashard are the same age. He's probably a little jealous that you had a family, and he didn't have anyone but you to stay with. To make matters worse, he had to sit around waiting, watching you get money before he was able to put anything in his pockets. Going through something like that is enough to make someone envious instead of appreciative."

Just as Tammy had finished speaking, the waitress brought their food to the table and sat their meals between them.

"What you're saying does make a lot of sense, but I always thought he and I were better than that. He always told me that we would be brothers for life because of the struggles that we went through together," K.Y responded somberly.

"He could tell you anything that he wanted to, but what were his actions saying? What it sounds like to me is that you held down a grown-ass man. He knew that if anyone would help him out, it would be you, and he took advantage of that. If he was your friend, he should have been concerned about bringing you new clients instead of figuring out exactly who you were already dealing with.

Anyway, while you were shelled up in that home of yours, I was productive and reached out to the restaurant owner. He showed me a clip of the tape, and I was able to see the figure of who it might be.

Why don't you set something up so I can meet him and help you find out if it was really him or not."

"You would do that for me?"

"Of course I would. I'll even do you one better, but it will take a little acting on your part. We are going to find out just how much of a snake your so-called friend really is."

CHAPTER SIX

It was a Friday night, and everyone who was everyone had shown up to K.Y.'s neighborhood bash. He had cooks on the grill making hamburgers and hotdogs for the neighborhood kids. He also had chicken, ribs, potato salad, macaroni & cheese, baked beans, and all kinds of alcoholic beverages for the adults to choose from. Although Florida was usually pretty warm all year round, the weather was finally nice enough for someone to just wear some comfortable clothes and have a good time outside without worrying about having a heat stroke.

Tammy let her hair that she typically kept up in a ponytail flow down today, and all of the curls were perfectly in place. She wore a sheer black cropped tee that stopped underneath her large breast and some high waist acid-washed shorts that cut off right below her ass. Her freshly manicured toes looked beautiful in her sandals, and the red lipstick she was wearing helped to bring out her sex appeal even more.

Tammy stood by the bar Kyle had set up, and she assisted the bartender in making drinks for the party-goers. She greeted everyone she met with a giant smile and made sure to engage in small talk with any friendly face willing to speak with her.

"Excuse me, shawty, I just want to introduce you to a friend of mine," K.Y. said as he took her hand to move her away from the drink she had been making.

"Hey, honey! This party is hot, and everyone around here just seems so nice."

"I'm glad you're having a good time, but I want you to meet my brother Rashard."

"Hey Rashard, I have heard so many things about you, so it's a pleasure to finally put a name with a face," she took his hand and pulled him in for a full embrace. She made sure to hug him tight and pull herself close to him when they hugged.

After she finally let him go, Rashard then responded. "Yeah, shawty, I heard bout you too. I'm glad he finally met someone who seems to care about him and where he is going with his life. From what I heard, he is fortunate to have met you."

Tammy tried to hide the fact that she was blushing. "I can't believe he actually had something nice to say about me. The way he acts with me, you would never have guessed he felt that way," she said while she jokingly slapped K.Y.'s chest.

"Well, maybe when you learn how to behave the way you're supposed to, you will be rewarded more often," he said in a stern voice. "This drink is nasty as shit. Make me another one and make it how I like it."

The smile that Tammy had was instantly gone as she took back the cup he handed to her. "I'm sorry. I'll go make it again. Did you want the same thing?"

"Obviously, I don't want the exact same thing because it tastes like shit. Use da same ingredients only make my shit good this time."

"Ok, daddy," she said before she walked off and headed back to the bar.

"Bruh! When you explained the shawty you was dealin' with, you didn't do her any justice. Dat bih is fine as fuck. Where da hell did you manage to find that one."

"She aight," K.Y stated. "I met her at her job when I went in to open a checking account."

"So she's fine, smart, and has a job of her own? It sounds like you definitely found a winner. Why you so rough with her, though?"

"I've been rocking with this bitch for a few months, and she still ain't let a nigga hit. I've dropped so much cash on this broad, and the way she is acting, you would swear she has gold between those thighs. She doesn't give it up when I'm nice or dropping thousands of dollars at the mall, so I'm trying a new approach to see if it works," he said with a light chuckle.

"You wild as fuck boy, but I see you. Sometimes you just got to put these hoes in check, but that don't sound like no hoe to me. The fact that she has her own proves she is already way better than some of these bitches that you usually mess with. I would be treating her differently if I were you," he responded.

"Come on, man. I don't mean anything by it when I say it, but you would first have to pull a broad like that to be able to tell me how to handle one," K.Y. laughed.

"Ok, you got that. I don't have a bitch like that yet, but you can believe that I will. I wouldn't have believed they actually existed if I wouldn't have met one in the flesh today."

"Well, they do. I think I might hold on to this one for a little while even though she isn't behaving quite like I want her to. Once she stops holding that back from a nigga, I might start treating her like I used to again. "

"Once again, I'm happy for you, bruh."

"I appreciate that. Do you think you can go over there and grab that drink for me? I think I just seen a possible problem walk in. I have to make sure that she isn't bringing any drama with her." Before he gave his friend a chance to answer the question, K.Y. was already walking toward a group of fine women. A few of the faces that the girl K.Y went to speak to was all too familiar to him because Rashard had already run through.

"Is K.Y's drink ready cause he is asking for it," Rashard asked Tammy.

She flashed him a wide grin before turning around to grab his drink. "Yeah, it's right here. I hope it's good this time because I really hate it when he acts like that."

"I'm sorry that my dude was talking to you so rough he isn't always like that."

"I appreciate you saying that, but unfortunately, I'm used to him acting like that now.

When he and I met, he was so sweet and romantic and just kind of changed up overnight. I'm not sure what happened because I thought we were good, but sometimes he goes through those mood swings. I try not to say anything because I know he's been under a bit of stress lately."

"That's sweet of you, but you still don't deserve to be treated that way. You seem like such a sweet and bubbly person."

"Thanks, that is so sweet of you. You seem like a great person also, which is why I'm so glad I got a chance to finally meet you tonight. I hope that we can meet up again soon and get to chat in an area where it's not so noisy."

"What did you have planned to do after this," Rashard asked her while looking her up and down.

"I'm not sure yet. I thought K.Y and I were supposed to be linking up later. But watching how he is acting with those hoes over there really has me reconsidering that decision," Tammy said, sounding very disappointed.

"Look, I honestly didn't want to say anything, but I have sisters, and I would hate to see any of them going through what you're going through now. Unfortunately, this is typical K.Y behavior. Obviously, he doesn't know what he really has in front of him, so instead of treasuring you, he is over there chasing the nastiest pussy in the room. Everyone in here has probably been in that girl at least once, so I'm not sure why he is wasting his time with someone like that when he could be over here romancing someone as beautiful as you."

Tammy turned her head quickly to hide the fact that his statement made her blush, but she didn't do it fast enough.

"What I'm saying isn't just words, shawty. It's all true. You're a queen, and you deserve to be treated like one. Like I tell my sisters, stop settling for bronze and go for the gold."

"I thought K.Y was your friend. How do you feel about saying stuff like this to me?"

"K.Y. has always and will always be someone that I love as a brother, but I can't always agree with his behavior and how he handles his business.

He has always had this kind of entitled behavior like he is supposed to have the best of everything. Because of that, he never really takes the time to appreciate what he has right in front of him—like with you, for example.

I work just as hard as that nigga, if not harder. Why does he get the queen when he isn't doing his job by acting as the king? He should have never had you over here making his drink, much less barking orders at you. He should have been the one catering to you while you had a chance to relax and mingle.

To be honest with you, he and I just talked about you, and I want to tell you what he told me, but I just don't want to hurt your feelings. You just seem like such a nice person."

"I promise I won't say anything at all to him if you just tell me. I would much rather know the truth before I end up doing something with him that I will regret later on," Tammy said.

"Well, he told me that you haven't given him the drawers yet, which is why he is even over there with them hoes now. He feels like if he can't get it from you, then he might as well get it from someone he knows will throw it at him.

Tammy looked genuinely hurt when Rashard shared those words with her. "I really considered becoming intimate with him. I can't believe he would say something like that after all I've done for him.

He likes to throw out the fact that he bought me a few pairs of shoes, but he forgets that I'm the one who showed him how to properly invest his money to have that much money to spend. I wonder how he will feel if I made his whole world come crashing down on him and fuck him over like he's trying to do me," Tammy huffed with anger. "He better consider himself lucky that because I am the way I am, I wouldn't even do him like that."

"I know you're upset, shawty, and sadly sometimes people just have to find out things the hard way."

Rashard and Tammy continued talking throughout the entire night. He told her his whole life story and even felt comfortable enough to share just how his mother had passed away.

"She was really into drugs, and OD'd one night. I was the one who found her, and I'll never get that memory out of my head. Even though she did her thang, she always looked out for me, and I tried to look out for her too. I regret not coming home at the time I promised her because maybe if I had, I could have saved her."

"It's not your fault Ra, so don't blame yourself. When it's someone's time to go back home, all we can focus on is the fact that they are now in a better place than we are. Now, she doesn't have to struggle with whatever she was using drugs to deal with.

"Ladies and Gentleman, this is the last call for alcohol, and this is also the last dance," the DJ called out through the mic. "I'm so glad that ya'll joined us for a nice peaceful evening of food and family fun."

"Oh my gosh," Tammy said after she looked at her watch. "I can't believe we have been talking for the last 4 hours. I really enjoyed talking to you and getting to know you."

"I did too. Hopefully, it doesn't have to end here. I want to get to know you better," Rashard replied.

"I would love to know you on a more personal note, but what about K.Y.," she asked.

"I really hate to see someone like you get played like you are right now. Why the fuck do you care about a nigga who isn't even willing to respect you? Just do you. Worry about what you want to do.

You're a big girl. You should be allowed to have friends, right? Let's keep our friendship between us. Cause what he doesn't know can't hurt him, anyway."

CHAPTER SEVEN

"I can't believe that fucking snake," K.Y screamed out once they were comfortable in Jason's studio later that evening.

"You need to dead him, and you need to do it now. Don't warn him or speak to him about anything. Just simply cut him off. If you don't do it and handle it the right way, I can promise you that you will end up paying for it later," Tammy stated.

"Yeah, young blood, that sounds like bad business," Jason co-signed.

"I've held that motherfucker down for years for him to treat me like this now. Who the fuck does he think I am?"

"Apparently, he thinks you're a sucker. He makes off with your product, and then he tries to get at me when you let him know that you're already interested in me. I will not repeat myself with this – cut him off!"

"I hear you, Tammy, and I will. I just want to be alone for a minute to sort through all of this. I'll get up with you guys later," K.Y. said before excusing himself.

Both Tammy and Jason remained absolutely quiet until they had seen K.Y. pull away from the studio from Jason's security camera.

"So you just pull a disappearing act? Where the hell have you been?"

"K.Y took a loss a couple weeks ago, and I handled business back home. You know what it is."

"That's definitely your old man's tricks," Jason chuckled.

"Well, I did learn from the best. I had to see what Kyle was going to do and how he would respond to it. I have to protect my business

54

too.

"I'm glad you're not as hardheaded as I always thought you were. It's clear you learned a few things through the years after all."

"Please don't remind me because those were some painful lessons to go through. I hate to be putting him through the tough love method of teaching, but it's been proven to work effectively."

"You know he really does seem to care about you," Jason said. "I've never seen him act like this with anyone. I haven't even heard him bring up another bird's name since he started dealing with you."

"Well, why would he mess with anyone else when he has someone like me in his corner," Tammy joked.

"You know there is a thin line between being conceited and confident. You really should learn it."

Tammy laughed, "I guess you're right. He's cool people, but he just still hasn't proven anything to me yet. I really need to see how he handles this situation with this Rashard character because that will speak volumes of how serious he takes his business."

"I guess we'll just have to wait and see what he does next," Jason said.

***

Tammy was on her way home when she received a call from K.Y. "I want to meet this chick and see if she wants to move in here. I want to move out of this place and into a new area. I would love to move someplace close to where you live."

"You have no idea where I live, so why would you make that statement," she said.

"You know that's right. You and I have been dealing with each other for months, and I still don't know where you lay your head. You know where I live, do my business, and you have seen where my connect lives. When do you give me the luxury of getting into your life more? I'm tired of having this major distance between us when I just want to be closer to you. It seems like whenever you and I get close, you pull away from me."

"I can't help it that I don't fully trust you. I can't deny that you and I have a type of chemistry which is why I have let you in more than I have ever let anyone else in, but I still need to see a few things from you."

"What else can you want from me? I give you prod-"

Tammy cut him off before he could finish his statement. "You sound absolutely foolish trying to talk to me like that over the phone. Meet me at the address that you've met me at before.

If you play your cards right, then maybe you'll finally get to find out where I lay my head and do my business," she said before disconnecting the line.

K.Y reached the complex in Windermere, FL, that was becoming a regular meet-up location for the two of them. It took him almost an hour to get there because he had driven on the other side of town to clear his mind.

Kyle waited for twenty minutes before he made an effort to call Tammy. *What the hell is taking her so long? She usually always waits for me in the front when she knows that I'm coming.* He thought.

K.Y called her eight more times before he realized that he had made a blank trip. *It's bad enough that she plays childish games with me, but this shit is getting ridiculous. Who the hell does she really think she is playing with me like this? I swear she knows exactly how to make me feel stupid for continuing to deal with her on a personal level.*

After waiting there for an hour, Kyle finally decided it was time to just head home. When he pulled in front of his driveway, he made sure to send her a text message to let her know exactly how he felt. "I don't know what twisted game you're playing with me, but I really don't enjoy wasting time just for your entertainment. Have great fucking night."

***

When Kyle woke up the following day, he saw that his iPhone had received a new message.

"I can't help it that my phone is not as fancy as yours. I didn't see any notification from you, so I just went to sleep."

Instead of texting her back, he made the decision to call.

"That's a really lame excuse," K.Y stated when she answered the phone.

"I don't know why you honestly believe I have any reason to lie to you. Maybe if I had an iPhone, I wouldn't have any issues receiving the messages you send to me."

K.Y had been laughing at her for months for her decision to use such a basic phone. He always made jokes that since it was the year 2010, she should have a phone with a full keyboard. But Tammy always said that she didn't find the need in having a phone with so many distractions when the only thing she needed her phone for was to make and receive calls. Lately, though, she had been missing out on a few opportunities because of her phone, and she knew it was time to finally get a new one.

"Why don't you meet me at the Florida mall for lunch, and we can talk about whatever you wanted to talk about last night. Then, we can see how much it's going to cost you to get you one of those phones," K.Y suggested.

For once in the 4 months that he had known Tammy, she didn't protest at his idea. She actually let him pick the meeting place and time and was there on time just like she always was.

The two of them enjoyed a simple lunch and afternoon just walking around and shopping the mall. Typically, Tammy made it known that all of the times they would meet up were business-related. But this time, it was personal. She never once stopped smiling, and K.Y couldn't get enough of that infectious laugh that she kept emitting from having such a good time with him. They never brought up the subject of business or money, and K.Y secretly wished they enjoyed more moments like this.

In the midst of having so much fun, K.Y didn't realize that he not only purchased the new iPhone for Tammy that she wanted, but he also bought her 5 outfits, shoes, and purses to go with everything.

"I'm taking you out to dinner tonight, so I can see one of those outfits on you that you just got," K.Y said as they strolled back to the car.

"I would love to, but I've got a few runs that I've got to take care of tonight," Tammy replied. "You know these bills don't pay themselves."

"You make so much money already, so I'm sure your clients won't miss you for one night."

"I've had a perfect day with you, and I would love to end it that way also. You know I don't play with my money, and since you don't pay any of my bills, you don't have any room to tell me what deals I can afford to take and which ones I can afford to miss," she snapped back in a matter of fact tone.

"I wanna treat you more like my woman and do things for you, but you're always making it known that you don't want help from me. That or you'll say you're not sure about me. Let's not forget how obvious you are about the fact that you have other options that you could be pursuing."

"I have to make sure that you're aware of that because otherwise, you will become complacent thinking that you are the one for me. You have been doing a good job of showing me some things, but it's going to take a lot more than just a few gifts to win me over. I can do things on my own. I can buy my own shit, pay my own bills, handle my own business deals, and do everything else in between by myself. Hell, I've even mastered getting off by myself," Tammy chuckled.

"My old man always told me that if a man doesn't treat me better than him, then I don't need him. He takes care of everything that I need, so why would I mess that up? I'm just going to take my time until I'm sure I've found what it is that I need in my life. Anyone can talk a good talk, but unless I've seen it supported by consistent action, it doesn't mean shit to me. I've heard it all before, but no one can seem to back up what the hell they say. Until that time comes, I'm fine by my damn self." Tammy placed most of her items in her car's trunk and then got into his vehicle's passenger side.

"What about your car," K.Y asked as she got in.

"Don't worry about it. I'll have someone else come grab it for me. For now, I guess I'll just enjoy this time with you, even though you were determined to try to ruin our day today."

He enjoyed seeing this side of her, but her comment made him feel uneasy. Normally, whenever she mentioned someone doing a favor for her, it was always another man. It bothered K.Y. that he was starting to feel jealous because no other woman had ever made him feel that way before.

K.Y.'s sudden uneasiness was apparent to Tammy, and she began to laugh.

"What the hell is so funny," he asked.

"You're so jealous with me," she said in between chuckles. "I've heard stories about you out here on these streets. You didn't think I knew about heartbreaker Kyle," she asked.

K.Y was a little embarrassed about his old nickname, but it was even more embarrassing that she knew it. "I've never denied my past to you. Before you came along, I never thought I would want to settle down because all I see out here are hoes just trying to get at my money, but you're different. It bugs me that you have other men doing shit for you that I'm perfectly capable of having done for you. Why don't you ever ask me to do shit like that for you? You never let me help you out."

"Sir, stop coming off insecure. Listen," she said as the laughter ceased. "I have other men doing shit for me, but they don't spend any quality time with me. They damn sure don't get to see the side of me that you do, so why does it even matter that they do what they think they need to in order to try to get to know me? If you don't want me to have other men doing shit for me, then step up and handle shit yourself. I don't like asking anyone to do a thing for me. If you want me to see you as a potential man, then why don't you just take care of business like a man is supposed to?"

"Shawty, there is a lot of things I want to do for you, but I just don't want to waste my time or money. What if, after doing all of this, then you just decide to be with someone else," he asked. "You also need to cut out the insecure comments cause I'm far from that," he said firmly.

"Well, you sure could have fooled me. The reason I don't worry about the flock of bitches that try to get at you daily is because I know none of those broads can fuck with me on my worst day, and I know that you know it too.

Anything that you do is an investment, and with any investment, you have to weigh out the risks and opportunities. Don't ask me any more dumb ass questions and instead ask yourself which one weighs more to you. Will you be risking more by shelling out a few pennies now and then and taking care of things for me, or will the opportunity of what can potentially happen be greater than what you might miss out on if I decided I'm sick of hearing you complain about shit not being what you want?"

K.Y paused a moment before answering her question. "I hear what you saying, and I guess it makes sense, but if I'm going to be handling my shit with you, then you need to dead those other niggas."

"I don't need to do shit but make money and die," she replied in a firm tone.

"The moment I see you are not selling me dreams is the moment I will cut off those men who have been holding things down for me for years. Until you give me a reason to take you seriously, I will continue to take this as I have been. I will continue to see you as a friend and business partner," she said. "Anyway, I need you to take me to my house so that I can grab something real quick."

K.Y had never been past the front sign of her community complex. He hoped that she would have invited him up so that he would be able to see what apartment she lived in, but he wasn't going to make an issue when she seemed to be warming up to him.

"These apartments look nicer up close," he said as she got back into his car. "That outfit looked good on the mannequin, but it looks even better on you," K.Y complimented her on the outfit that he had just purchased for her.

"If you think the apartments look good on the outside, you would be amazed to see what they look like inside," she said, giving him a sly grin.

"Well, too bad I wouldn't know because I never got my invite."

"I have been dealing with some dudes for years who don't even know what complex I live in, so you should be happy to know which building my apartment is even in."

"You keep baby feeding me information and telling me shit like that like it's supposed to make me happy," K.Y said as he made his annoyance evident.

"Let me guess," she started. "You have flocks of birds out there that would be dying to show you the inside of their crib and their walls," she chuckled.

"You can say it however you want to, but you know that's it's true."

"It doesn't matter how true the statement is because you're here with me. That lets me know that the quality of women you are dealing with is not my caliber. Maybe you should think before you speak because you make yourself appear stupid when you try to make weak points.

Hopefully, we can cut out the foolishness and get back to business. I'm going to do something I initially didn't want to do, and I'm going to include you in my plans tonight.

I've been having a few conversations with that rapper that you met with, and I think it's time that you met him for a face-to-face discussion."

I can't have you fucking up this deal for me, so instead of being a part of the meeting, you will simply make an appearance and drink. You will bring up the fact that I've done some successful deals for you in the past, which is why you trust me to handle all the paperwork and make your deals for you. That is it. Once he or I start talking about numbers, you will excuse yourself because I have something more important for you to take care of.

Ensure that when you excuse yourself from the table, you appear to be super busy with another business deal. I will be using your car this evening, and you will be going to pick up my car with your friend Rashard. He is going to meet you at the restaurant."

The sound of his old friend's name was enough to enrage K.Y., but he was even more pissed off that she had obviously had communication with him.

"Why the fuck you been talking to that nigga," K.Y spoke up. "I thought you told me to cut him off, so why you still speaking to him and dealing with him."

"I don't have to answer to no one, so the next time you decide to open your mouth, you really should reconsider the tone you speak to me in," she replied casually.

"After some reconsideration, I realized that it is best to find out what information he might know about you so that we can prevent future issues with him. While I'm having dinner with this dude, you will have Rashard take you to my car. While you are speaking to him, you want to maintain that same composure you did the last time you saw him. Make sure to bring up the loss you took a few weeks back and check out his response. How he reacts to what you say will tell you a lot about him. When you're speaking to him, make it seem like you have no idea that he and I even talked."

"How does that make any sense when you have me meeting him to pick up your car?"

"I sent him the text from your phone and told him that you were going to talk to him about money. Once he picks you up to get the car, give him a couple of dollars for his tank and tell him you'll be in touch with him soon."

"Well, what am I supposed to talk to him about?"

"Do I need to chew your food for you too," she asked, clearly annoyed. "I have figured out every last little detail, so the least you can do is figure out what wild goose chase you're going to have him on."

K.Y. pulled up in front of the restaurant, they both got out of the car, and he handed the keys to the valet.

"Scheme is already here and at the table waiting for me. We are going to walk up there together and have this drink and brief conversation. Rashard will be here in less than 20 minutes, and you need to be at the bar waiting on him before he has a chance to walk around the restaurant and see me sitting with Scheme. If you actually handle your business correctly, you might be rewarded generously," she said seductively.

The thought of being intimate with Tammy instantly caused K.Y. to become hard.

She giggled when she noticed what her suggestion had done to him. Before they had a chance to walk into the restaurant, she grabbed his hand and led him to the side of the building, where it was dimly lit.

Tammy put her back against the wall and pulled K.Y. close to her, and began whispering in his ear. "I'm as eager as you are to find out how you are in the bedroom, but I'm more interested in seeing how you handle your business. If you do this right, then I'll make sure that we have a good night." Before she pushed him away, she lightly bit his earlobe and caressed his erect penis with her hand. After fixing herself, she moved away from K.Y and went inside.

"Good evening Ms. Santiago and welcome back to Ned's," George, the host, greeted her. "The other party to your table is already here. Please follow me."

Tammy had really enjoyed coming to this restaurant. She enjoyed it so much that everyone from the owner to the gentlemen working the valet addressed her by her name.

When she reached the table, Scheme stood up and greeted Tammy by pulling her in for a small embrace and kiss on the cheek.

"I had a feeling you were going to be attractive, but I certainly wasn't expecting you to be as beautiful as you are," he said while he was taking his seat. "You're one lucky man," he told K.Y. as he shook his hand from across the table.

"Oh, please stop," Tammy said as she blushed. "I'm lucky to have such a smart and talented business mentor as Mr. Cole, and I have to agree I wasn't expecting you to be as good-looking as you are," she said with a smile. "Mr. Cole told me that you were a giant, but I didn't expect you to be so tall," she said, referencing his tall 6'8 stature.

"It's a pleasure to finally sit down and get a chance to meet you, man," K.Y said while masking his irritation with their blatant flirtation.

"I told Jason that I was looking for a solid investor to help me get things going in a different direction, and he told me that you were the one I needed to speak with. I know that anyone he recommends has to be good money, so the pleasure is all mine," Scheme replied. "I've already had a chance to talk with Ms. Santiago about where I see my business going. I also brought a copy of my business plan so that you guys can even take a look at it and tell me what you think."

"You can call me Tammy or Tee for short. We don't have to be so formal. It makes me feel old when someone calls me that," she chuckled.

"I'll call you Tee from now on then," Scheme said, turning his gaze over to Tammy.

Although K.Y. had been instructed to sit down and have a drink, he really didn't want to witness any more of the attraction that seemed to be evident from Tammy and Scheme.

He had been around Tammy for months, and she still would have an issue whenever he tried to call her by the nickname that only close friends and family called her by. After a few conversations and one meeting, he couldn't believe that she had allowed him the chance to be so close with her.

"As much as I would love to go over your business plan, I actually have another meeting to get to, and I really don't want to be late," K.Y. lied as he checked his watch for the time.

"It's too bad that you can't stay," Tammy uttered before turning her attention back to Scheme. "After speaking to you about your vision for your business, I can only imagine how this business plan is going to be."

"Well, I trust that you'll take care of everything as smoothly as you always have," K.Y. said to Tammy. He made sure to give a fake smile the moment he had an opportunity to interject. "You always make sure that business gets handled no matter what you have to do to get it done."

Tammy recognized his obvious sarcasm but simply replied, "Thanks, boss. I won't let you down. I'll make sure to handle all of the paperwork on this one like I always do."

Without responding to her, he turned to Scheme and said, "I hope you two have a wonderful evening, and I look forward to meeting you again soon." He shook his hand, stood up, and made his way to the bar.

K.Y. knew Tammy to be a businesswoman who never mixed business with pleasure. That's why it really bothered him to see her flirting so openly with someone she barely knew.

They had just previously had a discussion on his feelings, so he couldn't imagine why she would have dismissed his feelings so soon. *I'm sure she can accomplish anything she needed to with this nigga without having to be so disrespectful by flirting with him in my face.* K.Y thought to himself.

He ordered himself a drink at the bar and sat patiently as he waited for Rashard. *I have to spend the night with this fake ass bum while she's on a date with this nigga.*

K.Y fought the urge to look over at the table he had just been sitting at, but he couldn't help it. Every time he looked at their table, he could tell that she was enjoying the dinner with Scheme more than he wanted her to. She was constantly smiling, and he even witnessed her playfully touch his hand a few times while she was laughing.

He had only been at the bar for ten minutes, but he had already had four shots of Patron and 2 rum and cokes. *I don't know why I care so much about someone who doesn't care about me. She'll find out soon though that I'm just as valuable as she is. She over there flirting with this nigga like his tall, big ass don't look like Rick Ross.*

Just as he was about to get up to use the restroom, he spotted Rashard at the host's podium. So that he wouldn't get a chance to see Tammy bluntly disrespecting him, he decided to just meet him there and head out.

"What up, bruh," Rashard asked.

"Nothing, homie. I'm just ready to roll," K.Y replied somberly.

"Nigga, I just walked in, and I haven't had a chance to eat yet. Let's grab a table so I can finally figure out why everyone is always talking about how good this place is."

"I said let's roll because I'm ready to get the fuck outta here. The food is good, but you should have thought about that and came earlier if you was hungry," K.Y spat back.

"My nig-," before Rashard had a chance to get out the second word to his sentence K.Y spoke up in a thunderous tone.

"I said we're leaving, NOW," without saying another word, K.Y. exited the building.

Because he didn't know who was in the restaurant and didn't want to take the chance of anyone seeing him just get scolded by his own friend, he waited a minute before heading out.

"I don't know what your issue is, but I need you to remember that it's not with me.," Rashard retorted as he unlocked the driver's door to his beat-up 1999 Chevy Tahoe. "Just tell me where the fuck we going so I can drop your miserable ass off and go get something to eat."

"I'm not miserable, but I'm just not in the mood for bullshit right now." K.Y. was not a light drinker, but drinking so much so fast and on an empty stomach had him feeling his liquor already.

"You look like you're already fucked up," Rashard said, trying to change the subject and the tone of their conversation. "Is everything good?"

"Man, it's too much to even get into right now," K.Y replied

"With as long as you and I have been down for each other, you know I always got time. How many other niggas you think can hit me up an hour before they need to be somewhere and I show up this quick for them?"

"I took a big loss a few weeks back, and it's still been heavily on my mind. I'm so good to everyone around me, so I'm not sure why someone would be looking to harm my business when I make sure that everyone around me eats."

"Damn. I'm really sorry to hear that. What happened," Rashard asked.

"I was sitting at dinner eating when someone broke into my car and stole ten pounds."

"OH SHIT! Ten pounds of free product is enough to get someone on their feet. I would be mad about that shit too," Rashard replied.

"I was really out of twenty pounds because I had to replace the product that my customer had already paid for. This shit just doesn't make any sense to me."

"I been telling you that some of those niggas you was dealing with was flawed, but you don't hear me, though. You know good and well that when I was making runs for you, you never saw any kind of loss like that. Anyway, I'ma take you where you wanna go, but I really need to put some food in my stomach first," Rashard said as he pulled in front of a small establishment to grab some food. "Do you want anything while I'm in here?"

He shook his head to let him know he wasn't interested. *Maybe I should put something in my stomach because this alcohol hit me hard already.* K.Y thought to himself as he watched Rashard enter the building. *Pull yourself together, Kyle. You have a mission to complete and you're supposed to be playing this nigga close to see how much he knows and if he was even capable of setting you up. Don't start slippin' now.*

After several minutes, Rashard came out of the hole in the wall with just a sandwich and two drinks.

"That food is so good I ended up eating most of it inside. I brought us some drinks, though, since it's obvious that you trying to make it that kind of night."

"I really shouldn't have another drink because I'm already feeling the ones that I had back at the restaurant," K.Y countered

"Come on man, don't be a bitch! Back in the day, we use to kill bottles of Hennessy and Remy. Don't tell me ya ass can't enjoy a drink with your boy now cause you can't hold ya liquor," Rashard joked.

Even though he knew he shouldn't have another drink, he couldn't let his boy punk him for being a light weight. "Nigga give me that damn cup so I can remind you who the fuck K.Y is. I know it's been a minute, but it's obvious that you forgot about me."

"Yo, while we kicking it," Rashard started. "I wanted to let you know that I thought it was kind of foul how you did ya girl and how she did you.

You know me, and how I handle my business, so I'm just going to let you know the truth. I rapped a few words to her to see if she would be the type of female to deal with a nigga behind your back. That hoe is a fraud. She does a damn good job at playing that good girl role, but I know for a fact that I could have had her that night if I really wanted to."

"Why the hell would you say that," K.Y asked as he straightened himself up from the slump that he was in.

"That hoe wasn't even worried about you a few minutes into our conversation. She noticed you in the cut talking to Keisha and took it to be more than it was. I said a few things to her, just being me, and the hoe was all up in my face for the rest of the night.

You really should tell that hoe to kick rocks, bruh. That's not a good look for a nigga like you in these streets. You got a reputation to protect, and if niggas think they can rob you and get away with it, then your reputation is already slipping. We need to team up and remind these fools how shit is supposed to go out here."

K.Y became confused. He didn't expect Rashard to be so open with him about his attempt at Tammy. "I ain't been chillin' with shawty like that anyway," K.Y. lied. "I've just been focused on trying to recoup from this loss and get back on my feet."

"Good, and you should really keep it that way.

I've been working on my own little come-up, and I really want us to team up again like we use to in the past. Regardless of how these hoes try to act out here, they are all the same, and they all ain't nothing but trouble; some of them are just better at pretending than the other ones.

K.Y. never had any reason to doubt Tammy or her loyalty, so he wasn't sure why Rashard's words were affecting him so much now.

K.Y was already feeling a little sour about how she did him back at Ned's, and it didn't help with his friend talking so negatively about her. To stop thinking about Tammy and his feelings for her, he changed the subject.

"So what's this come up that you're working on," K.Y. asked.

"I just been working on some new clientele, is all. One of my boys just went away to school, and he said those niggas over there don't know shit about good weed. He's mad popular out there, so he won't have any problem helping us move the shit, so I figured that we could branch off and start making some money with the ones that's really trying to spend it. You know those college kids can't have a party without the green."

Although the alcohol had his brain in a daze, K.Y. liked what he was hearing. K.Y. considered himself a businessman and was always interested in ways to make more money.

Before he had a chance to reply to Rashard, they pulled into the parking lot where Tammy's vehicle was parked, and K.Y helped navigate him to the car.

"Aight, bruh," Rashard started as he put his car in park so his friend could get out. "Make sure you think about what I was saying because I think this could really be a good look and come up for us."

"Yeah, I am going to hit you up in the next couple of days about it so that we sit down and talk numbers," K.Y responded as he stumbled out of the car.

Once he was comfortable in Tammy's car, he pulled out his phone to send her a text. For the first time of the night, K.Y finally realized just how intoxicated he really was when he tried to type it up.

"I got your car. What now," he sent.

"Meet me by the Sheraton on International drive. Pay for a NICE room and have my key waiting for me at the desk," she responded almost immediately.

She might have flirted with that fool, but she's going to be with me tonight, K.Y. thought to himself as he put the car in drive and headed to have a good night with Tammy

***

K.Y. instantly became excited as he heard the sound of Tammy at the door, but he tried to play it cool. The drinks he had earlier and the alcohol he started sipping on in the room definitely had him feeling nice.

"I had a great night talking about and making money this evening, she said as she came in and put her bags on the table. " I can't wait to hear how your night went."

Tammy sashayed over to the bed and began to take her heels off when she suddenly smelt the vast amount of liquor that seemed to be pouring out of K.Y.'s pores.

"Are you drunk," she asked irritably.

"I had a few drinks over at Ned's, but it was only because you pissed me off," K.Y. slurred.

"With the way that you smell right now, there is no way in hell you only had a few drinks. Anyway, what the hell could I possibly have done to cause you to forget that you had a mission to accomplish tonight?"

"First of all," K.Y started as he got up from the bed. "Why the hell did you have to flirt with that motherfucker in my face? And why is it ok for him to call you by your nickname and not me?"

Tammy didn't immediately answer his question and instead started putting her heels back on. She walked over to the small table in the corner of the room, took a seat, and crossed her legs.

"I had a good night, and that's the only reason why I'm trying to not go the hell off on you right now. I suggest that if you want to keep it that way, then you'll sit your drunk ass down and remember who the fuck you're dealing with," she said firmly.

Once K.Y. did as he was told, Tammy continued to speak.

"In case your behavior isn't obvious, a large percentage of men can't seem to make good business deals with attractive women. Normally, one of two things is going to happen. Either he will think that if he makes his deal more enticing, he has a better chance of sleeping with her, or he's going to try to sleep with the woman for her to get what she wants from him. No matter how you look at it, most men will be thinking with their smaller head instead of the larger one," she said as she crossed her arms in front of her chest. "I simply beat him to it by allowing him no room for the second option. By letting him know I was already attracted to him, he would have no reason to think that trying to get me to sleep with him would work for me to get what I want.

From my attitude, he would know that to stay in my good graces and his shot at an invitation between my legs, he would have to continue to do things my way. Now, what exactly is it that you were complaining about?"

K.Y. instantly felt foolish. Instead of responding to her, he simply took a deep breath and hung his head down.

"I imagine that you were so drunk that you couldn't complete the one simple task I wanted you to accomplish this evening," Tammy asked.

"Well, while I was with him, he told me about him trying to get at you, and he also brought up what I think could be a good business deal. I think -," before K.Y could finish his sentence, Tammy fell into a fit of laughter.

The laughter ceased almost as soon as it started, and then she spoke up in a clearly agitated tone. "Did you or did you not complete the one simple task I asked you to do today? I didn't ask you to provide me with any of that other bullshit you just tried to sell me with. I asked one simple question that required a yes or no answer."

"Yes, but I -"

"Ok so then if you accomplished the mission why was he able to sell you on a potential business deal instead of you having a report on your findings from him," she asked.

After a few minutes of silence, she began speaking again. "I am actually really interested in hearing what this idiot could have said that would have made you forget the whole reason why you were even with him tonight."

"He has a friend who goes to college who wants to get some product to start moving at his school. He explained that his boy is really popular out there and could help us expand to reach more customers. I think -"

"In case you haven't realized by now, I have no desire to hear what you think. To me, it's all stupid!" Tammy took a deep breath to calm down before she continued. "Let me get this straight. Dummy number 1 tells dummy number 2 that they should expand their business. Can you please fill me in on what business dummy number 1 owns," Tammy asked.

"After I told him about how I lost the ten pounds and had to practically give away another ten, he thought that -"

"Why the hell did you tell him how much product you lost," Tammy asked while again cutting him off. "Why wouldn't you tell him you took a loss and leave him with a potential opportunity to tell on himself? Now he knows that not only can you afford to take a ten pound loss, but you had enough product lying around to just give away more. You just let that motherfucker know that you're no longer just moving baby weight anymore. If he couldn't guess before by your fancy car, phone, and clothes, then he knows now that you have more than just a couple dollars in your pocket. You hardly see the man make any real moves for himself, but the moment he finds out what you're moving, he has potential business deals." Tammy began to chuckle at how naïve K.Y had been with Rashard.

"I no longer have any desire to know what you two idiots could have possibly discussed this evening. You're naïve, stubborn, impulsive, and you clearly cannot think for yourself.

If this fool that you have never met before in your life happened to get caught or get snitched on, he could get charges for the amount of product he has on him, the bag that the product is in, the scale that he'll need to weigh out the product, the bags that he'll need to place the product in to individual customers, and the list could go on. How many college kids do you think are ready for that kind of time? Let's not forget that he will also lose any potential scholarships, government grants, government student loans, and any other kind of government assistance that he could be receiving. Do you really think a kid wouldn't be willing to drop a few names in exchange for not having to take so much heat?"

"I never thought about all of that. I just thought that -"

"You never think anything all the way through. You never see the bigger picture because you're so busy in the moment," Tammy stood up, grabbed her purse, and placed the straps on her shoulder. "It's a shame that you couldn't do this one thing correctly," Tammy said as she lifted the Armani dress she was wearing to show off the all-black lace lingerie that she was wearing underneath. It left nothing for the imagination, and for the first time, K.Y was able to see just how perfect her large breast really were. To be so large, they sat up nice and perky even without her wearing a bra.

"I was really in the mood to finally release some of this pent-up stress and aggression since it's been so long." Tammy sat at the edge of the table and placed her foot on the arm of the chair to reveal that she wasn't wearing any underwear. She put two fingers inside of the lips of her vagina and began playing with herself. Even though he was on the other side of the room, he could hear just how wet she had been from all of the noise that was being made as she played with herself.

"I wanted to finally see what it would feel like to have you inside of me," she whispered in between her moans.

K.Y sat frozen as he watched Tammy please herself. "You can still find out," he said almost eagerly.

"Negative," Tammy replied as she placed her foot on the floor and fixed her clothing. "Until you learn how to handle business like the King you are, you won't even be able to taste my pussy, much less find out how it feels." She took the same two fingers that she had used to please herself and stuck them in her mouth and sucked and licked on them while maintaining her gaze on K.Y.

She grabbed her keys and headed for the door. "I purchased some condoms, food, and clothing because I thought we were going to be in here for a few days, but we won't. Jason will be in touch for my order and the $200 you owe me for wasting my money on stuff that I no longer need now." Without another word, she left K.Y. alone in the room, drunk, horny, and miserable.

CHAPTER EIGHT

It had been a month since K.Y had last seen Tammy that night in the hotel room. She stopped answering his calls, and she even changed her phone number. Just as she had in the past, she had Jason taking care of all of her orders, and although he tried to play it cool, the space between the two of them was killing him.

He tried to kill all of his free time by working out and spending more time in the streets making money. Being around all of his boys would help during the day, but going through what felt like his first heartbreak was difficult.

K.Y was on his way to Jason's studio to make another drop for Tammy. It seemed like whenever she was not dealing with him, her orders would double if not triple. *At least I know she's working and not out with someone else*, K.Y would tell himself whenever he was taking care of her orders. As he had always done, he pulled in the front space and got out to get her work for the week out of his trunk. Just as he had slammed his trunk shut, he noticed her Toyota Camry pulling out of the side alley next to the studio.

K.Y wanted to try to catch up to her before she pulled onto the busy street. But he knew it wouldn't be wise to do that because he needed to get this product inside away from anyone who might have been watching him.

"What up, young blood," Jason greeted his boy as he walked into the studio.

"Nothing, man, just busy working. Was that Tammy that left here before I came in," K.Y. asked.

"Come on, you know it was her," Jason replied.

"I don't have much time," K.Y lied. "I'm getting ready to take care of some other business. All the product she asked for is there, but I also threw in an extra pound for her."

Although it was a clear kick to his ego that Tammy was clearly avoiding him, he couldn't stop caring about her. He was still doing whatever he could to get her attention again.

"I'm sure she'll be happy to know that," Jason said with a smile.

"Well, when I try to tell her my feelings, it doesn't seem to work, so I'm hoping this will be enough to get her to call," he replied lugubriously.

"I know she's a problem, but it's all for a good reason. If Tammy made the decision to stay away from you, it's because she feels like it is best either for you or for her."

"Who the hell is she to try to tell me what's best for me? How the hell is leading someone on just to bounce when you feel like helping out the situation?"

"Obviously, the space that she has given you hasn't been enough for you to really think about why she pulled away from you in the first place.

Tee and I are cool, but we don't really talk about anything that's not money-related. She told me a little bit about what happened, and she also told me that she feels like you have a little maturing to do. Take this time to just worry about you, man. Go mingle with some people and build your clientele up. Why don't you even look into starting a business or something? Do something productive with this time instead of just sitting around angry because she's doing something she feels like she needs to do for the larger scheme of things.

I'm going to make sure that she knows the extra amount is a gift, but I can't promise that will be enough to get you any different results with her."

K.Y. gave his boy a pound and left the studio without another word. He went straight back to his house to take his boy's advice.

He walked into the house and hung his keys on the same hook he always did and walked straight over to his computer desk. He sat there in the dimly lit home while he pondered what he could possibly do to better himself and his chances with Tammy. Kyle hated to admit that besides hustling, he didn't know what else he wanted to do with his life. He spent so many of his early years focusing on being the best hustler in Orlando that he never really gave anything else a try. As he was beginning to get frustrated, an unknown number began calling his phone. Normally Kyle hated answering unknown calls, but he decided to answer it since he hoped it was Tammy.

"I appreciate the love you showed me. You know exactly how to make my day," Tammy's cheerful voice came through his phone.

"I figured it was the least that I could do. I've been thinking about you a lot, and I really miss -."

"Oh, cut it out," Tammy interjected as the tone of her voice hardened. "If you missed me or the time we spent together at all, you would have been doing what you should have been doing when I was around to give me a reason to want to stay. You simply miss my presence now because I'm not available to you at all."

"After all of this time, you didn't think about me or miss," K.Y asked, hurt by her response.

"I never said that, but if that's what you want to assume, I can't make you feel otherwise. You seem to be way too caught up in your feelings to handle business properly, and I can't afford to take chances or losses. I've been doing this a lot longer than you have, and I can't let your feelings get me caught up. I've done my research on you, and the fact that you're not clean tells me that you're clearly not as talented in this as you think you are," she snickered.

K.Y. had been arrested a few times in the past, but luckily he was never caught with a large amount of product. In the past, he was picked up while smoking with some friends or making a small run for a customer.

"So how is this genius business deal going with your boy," Tammy asked him sarcastically.

"There hasn't been a deal. I thought long and hard about what you said, and everything that you were saying made sense. I haven't hit him up, and I don't respond when he calls."

Tammy's end went quiet for a minute before she responded.

"I knew calling you back was a terrible idea," she said. "This man now probably feels used, and like you were just selling him dreams. If your boy was mad enough to possibly take something so petty from you, don't you think it would upset him that you're in a position to help him come up, but now you're flat out refusing to?"

"I get it. You're way more experienced than me, and it's obvious that I need your help because I'm not as good as I once thought I was.

Can we just try to move past this and go back to how we were?"

"If I hadn't called you to talk business, I would have hung up on you just now," she paused for a few seconds before she continued. "I need you to find someplace else to stay because that girl I told you about is ready to move in there. I want her moved in by December 1st, so you have two weeks to make shit happen. I need you to pack up all of your valuable shit into a moving van. Once you're all done with that, park the van in the alley behind Jason's studio. Once that's done, I'll know that you're ready to move on to the next step," after she was finished speaking, Tammy disconnected the line.

Kyle sat still for a few moments. He hated that she was so in control of their situation. He was also beginning to dislike himself for not having the balls to just leave her the fuck alone.

I wish I could just forget I ever met her and move on with my life, he thought. As easy as that sounded to him, he knew that it would never be possible to just forget her and move on.

When Kyle was younger he had been known to have a 'love them and leave them' kind of attitude with the women that he had dated. *Maybe this is my karma for how fucked up I had been with hoes in the past. I finally open my heart up to a female, and it seems like she couldn't give a rat's ass. There are so many chicks out there that would beg me to give them half of the amount of effort that I give Tammy, but she doesn't give a damn. I just don't get it.*

After sitting in that spot thinking for at least an hour, he finally thought it was time to get up and get shit done.

He looked through the small house he grew up in and tried to see if he could find anything of value he wanted to take. When his mom started using cocaine, she made sure to get rid of everything of value that they had. She sold their TVs, DVD players, jewelry, and just about every electronic that they owned.

K.Y knew it was time to get out of the house that he had spent so many years in, but he just couldn't shake all of the happy memories that he had shared with his mom.

Although she was a single mother, she had always made sure that he and his two siblings were taken care of. She worked long and hard hours as a Certified Nurse Assistant, but she only ever earned enough money to keep bills barely paid for, food on the table, and clothes on their backs. When Rashard moved in when he was only sixteen, things became more difficult to keep up with.

Kyle had been in the streets for four years, but he was only making chump change by making small runs for his uncles. The money he made in a month was barely enough to pay for their utilities, but he figured every little bit could help.

Kyle walked into the kitchen one morning while everyone else in the house was asleep to find his mother crying over a stack of bills.

"Kyle, Mama gon' have to get another job to keep everything going in here," she said in her thick country accent. "I'm not proud of it, but sometimes as parents, we have to do what we need to for stuff to be taken care of," she said in between sobs.

"I'm going to need you to be a big boy for me and take care of your siblings for me at night because I'm not going to be here. I noticed that you've been coming into this house later and later at night, and as helpful as you're trying to be, I just can't have you out here on dis block no more. If any of us should be in these streets, it needs to be me," her last statement made her begin to cry all over again.

Kyle hated to see his mom like this. The only reason he had been up so early is because one of his boys told him about how much money could be made in selling cocaine instead of just weed. For the past 3 months, Kyle had saved his money to buy some product and work it himself. Now, he regretted holding back that money as he watched his mother sob incessantly. He walked over to her and wrapped his arms around her to try to bring her some comfort.

"I'm heading out to work, and I need you to stay here to get breakfast and lunch started for your siblings. I won't be home tonight, and you probably won't see much for the rest of the weekend. I'll be home Monday morning since I'll be off from the hospital. I promise then I'll be able to free you up so you can get to enjoy being a kid again," she gave him a kiss on the forehead. Then, she went into her room to change.

Kyle was too young and naïve to understand exactly the extra job his mom was about to take on. Still, he loved his mother and was willing to do anything that she needed him to do in order to help take care of the family.

Kyle did as his mom asked and prepared breakfast, and he also cleaned and seasoned the chicken that he was going to cook later. After he saw his mom out, he woke up his siblings and helped get them ready for school.

Kenya and Kennan, his 10-year-old siblings, were twins. He asked Rashard to run them over to the elementary school so that he would be free to go handle business himself.

"Why I got to be stuck with yo baby brother and sister while you get to go do da fun stuff," Rashard asked irritably.

"Just do what da fuck I asked you to do. Once dis gets popping, there will be plenty of time to do da fun stuff together, but I need to get us on first. The man I'm finna go see today don't know you. Hell, he hardly knows me, but he's going on the strength of one of my boys. I don't have much money to grab anything large, but if we do dis right, we will be able to come up soon anyway.

Everyone on the block has been telling me that moving coke is where all the real money is. This is a new area for us, so we are going to have to move smarter when he do make any moves," Kyle said, meaning every word of it.

Even though Rashard didn't want to do what his friend had asked him to do, he knew that Kyle could be stubborn when he was ready. He didn't see any reason to try to fight him on something that he already seemed so firm about.

In the time it took Rashard to take his siblings to school, Kyle had met with his dealer and grabbed the product that was helping his boys come up. Kyle was young and inexperienced. He didn't realize his dealer's price was overpriced. Kyle started this to take care of his family, but his dealer felt like his next come-up would come from the young man's ignorance.

Kyle was anxious to prepare his product and get it in the streets, but he knew that his mom had left him with specific instructions to help out in the house while she was out. Kyle had always felt like he was the man of the house since he was the oldest one living there. Since his mother just confirmed his position, he wanted to take on the role more seriously.

Kyle stayed home from school that day and made a few runs with Rashard while they waited until 3:00 PM to pick his siblings up from school.

The rest of the night went smoothly. The four kids had a great night eating Kyle's home-cooked meal, watching movies, and playing a few board games. Kyle put his siblings to bed at their regularly scheduled time and sat in the living room for the rest of the evening watching TV.

It was three in the morning when he heard keys at the front door. Kyle instantly became nervous since his mother said she would not be returning for the rest of the night.

The person at the door fumbled to unlock the door for a full three minutes before they were able to get inside. By that time, Kyle had enough time to run into his mother's room and grab the bat that she kept in there for their protection.

The stench of alcohol and promiscuousness danced through Kyle's nostrils before he even had a chance to see that it was his mother and some unknown man at the door.

"I'm so sorry, baby. I had no idea that you woulda been up at dis time," his mother slurred as she tried hard to keep her balance. "Dis here is my friend, and he just wanted to make sure that I got home safely. Why don't you run off to bed, and I'll see you later," she said as she blew him a kiss and headed hand in hand for her bedroom with the unknown friend that had been with her.

This was the first time Kyle had ever seen his mother drunk, and it was undoubtedly the first time that he had ever seen his mother bring home anyone with her.

To add insult to injury, he had never seen his mother dressed so inappropriately. Even after three children, Sasha Cole had what men considered a coke bottle shape. He always respected that she never played off of her beauty alone. She had always told him, "A woman ain't a woman because of what she wears or looks like; it's all in what she knows." It disgusted him to see his mother wearing a tiny halter top, mini skirt, heels, and leather jacket.

Although she had asked him to go to bed, he didn't feel right being on the other side of the house with some stranger locked in a bedroom with his mother.

He turned down the TV and tried to fall asleep on the couch.

"Yes, daddy," he heard his mother call out. "Touch me right there," she moaned, not even trying to keep her voice down.

The sound of his mother having sex with the scumbag she brought home made Kyle's stomach turn, and he decided that he no longer wanted to hear any more of it. He put on his sneakers, woke up his friend, and decided to go down the block to see what was going on.

"Yo, Kyle," one of the neighborhood kids screamed out almost as soon as his sneakers hit the street pavement. "What's up wit ya momma?"

Kyle was already frustrated and was not in the mood to hear any slick remarks from anyone. He certainly wasn't in the mood to listen to anyone talk about his mom.

"I never seen Ms. Cole's sexy ass wear no shit like the outfit she just had on. That shit looked sexy as fuck. Your mom's pretty black ass can get it as long as her price is right," after that last comment, the group of boys that Drew, one of the boys who lived on the same block as Kyle, made everyone fell into a fit of laughter.

"Fuck you and your bum ass, Drew. You could never have a shot at my mama."

"Nigga anyone with a few dollars in they pocket got a chance at yo mama now. Don't be surprised if after I beat her down with dis sweet dick and I end up being yo new stepdaddy," again his jokes caused the young boys on the block to double over in amusement.

Kyle immediately wished he would have just stayed home instead of bringing his ass in the street to hear everyone talking shit. Drew was at least five deep, but he couldn't lose the respect of the block by allowing him to talk so recklessly about his mother.

"Bitch, the only one who is going to get beat is your ass if you keep talking out of the side of ya neck like that," Kyle responded, walking in the direction of where the young boys were standing.

"Why you wanna fight me when ya momma is da hoe," Drew responded, trying to withdraw from the apparent attempt Kyle just made to fight. "You need to be checking on her instead of worrying about the jokes we out here crackin' on you.

I heard that trick yo momma just took into yo' house don't like repaying his debt at the end of a service. You need to save your energy to beat that nigga off yo momma once he's done catching his nut from her freak ass."

Kyle really wanted to beat Drew's ass, but didn't want to take the tip he gave him as a joke.

"What you tryna do bruh," Rashard asked, letting his friend know that he was down to do whatever.

"Fuck these bums," he replied to his friend. "Drew, you gon' see me about this, and luckily for you, it's not tonight. You just better watch yo' ass because when I see you, I'm gon' fuck you up on sight," Kyle turned and headed back in the direction of his house.

K.Y. and Rashard snuck back into the house and sat quietly on the couch. As much as he was not interested in hearing his mom's wild escapade, he didn't want to take the chance that Drew might have been right in what he was saying.

Rashard fell asleep after sitting there in the dark for twenty minutes, but Kyle stayed up and alert in case anything popped off. He was tired, angry, and embarrassed as he sat through the longest two hours of his life listening to his mom say some of the nastiest shit he ever heard.

"I left yo money on the dresser," he heard the deep voice say as the man's voice got closer to the bedroom door.

"Wait motherfucker. I need to count dat shit before you go because I've heard about your reputation. This pussy ain't free, and I didn't do what I just did for you to try to cheat me out my damn money."

After a minute of silence, he heard his mom start speaking again, "Good boy. At least you know what bitches you can try and which ones you can't. Now get your black ass outta my house, and keep your noise down so you don't wake my fuckin' kids."

The man did exactly as he was told. He headed straight for the front door and was careful enough not to make another peep.

He heard his mother get into the shower and took the longest shower he had ever heard her take. His mom was always adamant about keeping showers down to a minimum to save on her water bill. But that didn't seem to matter to her tonight.

After locking the front door and listening to the water run for forty minutes, Kyle finally drifted off to sleep.

Not even an hour later, Kyle was awakened by the sounds of his mother getting ready for work. After changing into her scrubs, Kyle watched from the corner of his eyes as his mother dragged herself to the kitchen to make herself some coffee.

Kyle wasn't ready to face his mother about all that had transpired the night before, so he pretended to be asleep as he secretly watched every move she made.

"Lord please forgive me," he heard his mother whisper while she sat at the kitchen table. "I'm doing the best I can. I know you ain't put me on dis earth to do dis kinda work, but I got children to take care of," just as she had finished praying for forgiveness, he heard his mother sobbing again.

"I'm just so tired, Lord. I have no idea how I'm gonna get out of dis situation, much less last the rest of dis weekend."

Sasha finished her coffee, grabbed her bags, and walked over to the couch to give Kyle a kiss before heading out for her day job.

"Kyle, I left a list of things I need you to do for today. I'm sorry about last night. I love you," she whispered gently into his ear.

"Mmmm-hmmm," was the only response K.Y gave her.

"I guess I deserve that," she said. "My actions don't make sense to you now, but one day they will."

The rest of the day, Kyle was up in a cloud. The perfect life as he knew it was changing, and he knew that this was only the beginning.

Normally, his siblings would have been at the sitter's, and he would be allowed to relax at the house and do whatever the hell he wanted to. Now that his mother had to cut every expense that she could, he would now be the primary caretaker for his siblings. And he was quickly becoming tired of it.

Keenan and Kenya didn't require much because they were both intelligent and independent. Still, Kyle didn't want to be in the house watching kids when he could be in the streets making money.

"It's only eight o'clock. I'm not ready to go to bed yet," Kenya protested when he instructed his siblings that they would go to bed two hours earlier than they did on the weekends.

"People in hell want ice water, and I want a million dollars; we don't always get what we want," Kyle replied, not hiding his attitude at all.

Once he was sure that both kids were in bed and sleeping soundly, he and Rashard were back on the streets.

"I got a bad feeling in my gut about leaving those two brats home by themselves," Rashard said as they were turning the corner to leave Kyle's street.

"You probably just gotta take a shit," Kyle replied with a laugh. "I don't have no damn kids, and I shouldn't be forced to sit at home raising any either. I got shit to do and money to make."

The two boys were on their way up to one of their friend's house when they noticed a woman who favored Sasha standing next to the neighborhood bar with a small crowd of men around her.

"I'm on one and ready to fuck but only for the motherfucker that's willing to spend the most and ready to prove he has it," the young boys heard the woman say.

Kyle decided to keep walking because he wouldn't be able to face finding out the truth of what his gut was telling him. Drew was right, and his mother was now one of the neighborhood prostitutes.

"Hey K.Y.," Stacy, a young prostitute, said sexily. "What you two doing tonight.""

Not you," Rashard laughed.

"Boy, please! You wish you could afford to fuck with someone like me," she shot back to Rashard. "K.Y can I talk to you for a second," the young girl asked.

Stacy was bad, but everyone and their mama knew what she was about. "If you ain't paying, then you damn sure ain't playing," would be her response whenever any of the boys in the neighborhood tried to get at her.

"Anything you got to say to me you can say with my boy present," he replied flatly.

"Well," she started. "You guys know what I do, and I don't hide it from no one cause I ain't ashamed of it, but I'm just worried about yo mama. She isn't built for this life like she thinks she is."

"What is that supposed to mean," K.Y asked

"I saw yo mama up here with some of the other hoes, and to just be two days into this shit, she is already depending too much on that stuff to help her through her tricks."

Kyle knew exactly what she meant by her statement but couldn't believe that to be true. His mother had always warned him about the importance of staying away from drugs. Once Rashard's mother died of an overdose, she sat them down and explained why it was important for them to remain drug-free.

"I tried warning her about who she hanging wit, but of course she don't wanna hear it from a youngin like me. Those hoes don't want to lose their tricks or da money that those motherfuckers bring. Yo mama wants to believe that these hoes are trying to help her when they really want to get her out of this game faster than she started."

Kyle was instantly enraged. "Thanks for the tip Stace," he said just before he crossed the street.

As he got closer, there was no denying that the woman standing there in knee-high boots and obvious lingerie was his mother.

"What the fuck you doing out here like dat," K.Y asked furiously.

"Damn bitch, you better get outta here with dat crazy ass pimp. Don't nobody want any problems with the little man," the men began snickering at the old drunk's comment.

"Boy what the hell you doing out here, and why the fuck you worrying about my damn business," Sasha asked with her hand on her hip. "Take yo black ass home and do what da fuck I left you doing."

No matter how upset Sasha would be at Kyle, she never talked to him like that. Kyle didn't know what to do, but he knew that he didn't want to see his mother like this anymore.

Once she saw that the boys were not leaving, Sasha decided to take the party back inside the building.

"Daddy, do you think I can get a little bit more of the candy," she asked one of the men standing around her.

"Bitch, you've had enough free candy," the man replied. "If you want any more of this shit, it's going to cost you."

Sasha stopped in her tracks and became upset. "I already gave you money for the last one. Give me some more now before I get my kids to fuck you up."

"I suggest you listen to them kids tell you to take yo ass home because you've clearly had too much to drink and way too much candy. This shit was only supposed to help you make it through the night. Nobody intended for you to be high as a kite off of dis shit," the man responded.

Kyle couldn't take hearing any more of this conversation. "Sasha Cole, what the fuck are you doing? What happened to the woman that carried herself with dignity and self-respect," he asked while he took all of his strength and grabbed his mother by her arm. "I'm taking your high ass home. It's bad enough that you out here. How the hell are you going to turn around and spend the money you're making on drugs," he screamed out.

Sasha didn't hesitate or put up a fight and allowed K.Y to begin to tug her in the direction of their house.

"Can I please just get a little bit to go home with," she asked again as her anger turned to desperation, and she began to beg.

Instead of answering her, the men walked back into the bar laughing at her expense.

Although it wasn't a far walk back to the house, the journey seemed to take forever. The three of them made their walk back to their destination in complete silence. Once they were all safe and sound in the comfort of their home, Kyle finally broke it.

"The woman I thought was a prime example of the morals and values she tries to teach me is nothing more than a coked-out whore," he snapped angrily. "Any other day, you would have played those idiots for trying to talk to you, and now you're begging them for drugs while you're in your drawers."

"Boy let's get one thing straight," Sasha started. "I am still yo mama and you will talk to me with respect like you got some damn sense. I'm not proud of the decision I made to go back on the words that I've

"Boy, let's get one thing straight," Sasha started. "I am still yo mama, and you will talk to me with respect like you got some damn sense. I'm not proud of the decision I made to go back on the words that I've taught you, but sometimes in life, you have to do what you don't want to in order to get what you need. I got four damn mouths to feed, clothe, and provide shelter for. Now, that shitty job of mine decided to cut my hours instead of letting me work the overtime I was working before."

She grabbed the cheap bottle of vodka that she had in the freezer and three shot glasses. She filled them all up and drank them just as fast as she had poured them before she began talking again.

"I needed a little bit of that stuff to keep me up and take me through the night. It's bad enough that I don't want to do it, but some of these motherfuckers will really wear you out," she said, supplying Kyle with way more information than he wanted to hear. "I love all of my children, and that's the reason why I'm willing to make this kind of sacrifice to make sure that you all never have to go without like I had to. A real woman will always do whatever is necessary to make sure the people closest to her are straight."

"You can say whatever is goin' to help you sleep better at night, but you're a cheap prostitute who is out there begging for booger sugar from bums in front of the cheap ass neighborhood bar. If you cared at all about the people close to you, then you would have had enough respect to do your hoe shit somewhere else. Now, niggas think they can clown me on the block cause anyone can afford my mother's old ass pussy," he shouted.

"If you wake up my damn babies to this bullshit you talking, I will give yo' ass a beating that you will never forget," Sasha fired back as she slurred each word more than the one before it.

Before Kyle had a chance to respond, Rashard had returned to the living room with a blank stare on his face as if he had seen a ghost.

"They're not here," he said meekly.

"What the fuck is you talking 'bout," Sasha said as she stumbled in his direction.

"Kenya and Keenan are gone."

CHAPTER NINE

The sound of Waka Flaka's "Hard in the paint" came through the speakers of his iPhone and awakened Kyle from the deep nightmare he had been reliving.

"I'm mad at you, but I do kind of miss seeing your face," Tammy said.

"Why is it so hard for you to try to be nice to me," he asked, hoping that she would offer him some sort of relief. He needed that more than anything at that moment.

"It's because you constantly do stupid shit. Do you think I honestly want things to be this way between us," she asked. "I do have better things I could be doing besides arguing with you."

"I'm sure you do because you seem to have been very busy these last few weeks."

"I have been because I want to get away soon. I'm ahead with all of my work, and I just want to go enjoy a few days outside of Orlando, but I just don't have anyone to enjoy it with," she replied.

"Was that your way of inviting me to join you for your getaway," he asked sheepishly.

"Hell no," Tammy replied with a laugh. "That was, however, an indication that I'm willing to accept a sponsored vacation if someone is up to it.

Kyle didn't hesitate to reply, "When do you want to go and where are we going."

"I'll let you be in charge this time on when we're leaving, but I don't want to go anywhere too far. It's only going to be for a couple of days."

"Well get ready and meet me at the mall in an hour. I've got to head out and make a quick run. Then, we can go grab you some things, so we can leave tonight."

***

Kyle was eager to make this drop so he could quickly get to Tammy. Even though she could be a pain in the ass, he could tell little changes in her that proved to him that she was coming around.

In the time they had been dealing with each other, they had never done anything sexual. That made him even more attracted to her. She was sexy but never depended only on that. Her body was banging, but her confidence and class made her even more appealing.

His iPhone's vibration caused him to snap back to reality and remove himself from the daydream he had been in with Tammy.

"Hurry up and get here because you know I don't like to wait," Tammy said anxiously.

"I'm moving quickly, but I just got to finish this drop at the usual spot," he replied. "If I run a little late, I'll just make sure to get you something really nice to make up for it."

"So I guess this space is working after all because that was the smartest thing I've ever heard you say," she replied with a giggle. "Meet me at the outlet mall in the Armani store; I'm starting my tab in an hour," she said before the line went dead.

Kyle was already rushing. But knowing that he only had an hour before she would start spending his money caused him to start driving faster than he was already going.

He pulled up in front of Jason's studio and parked his car in the same spot that he always did. He got the product from the trunk, knocked on the door so that Jason could buzz him in, and walked inside the always dimly lit hallway.

Kyle had been so caught up in his daydream and rushing to get to Tammy that he had never paid attention to the two unknown men who had been following him ever since he left his home. The two men slipped into the building with ease before the door had a chance to slam shut and used the poorly lit vestibule to their advantage.

The first one into the building hit Kyle in the back of the head with such a large amount of force that he instantly fell to the ground.

"Don't do anything stupid," one of the men said in a deep, hushed, voice as he stood over Kyle. "We just want what you have on you, and we will let you keep your life."

Once Kyle realized what was happening, he attempted to reach his hip to grab his protection. Before he could get to his gun, the other man took the butt of his pistol and struck him several times as if he were using a tomahawk. The pain from the forceful blows left K.Y momentarily disgruntled. The two men continued to beat on K.Y even though they had already retrieved the items they were beating him for.

As much as he wanted to fight off his two assailants, their quick and fierce attacks were too much for him in his vulnerable position. K.Y did the best he could to block their hits until his body went limp.

***

"Who the hell taught you how to fight," K.Y heard Tammy's question faintly as he regained consciousness. "Everyone knows that you have to take out at least one of your aggressors with you."

"What the hell happened? Everything on me hurts."

"You got your ass whooped is what happened. I can understand not wanting to remember a beating like that either," Tammy replied with a laugh. "I'm sorry," she said as she tried to silence her giggle. "I know it's not funny, but you have to see the humor in this."

"I don't get it. I remember being attacked, but how did you get here so fast, and where are we going?"

"Kyle, you've been out for the past two hours. As soon as Jason called me and told me what happened, I rushed over to make sure that you were ok," she replied with sincere concern. "I figured that after what you just went through, you might still want to get away on this vacation. I had Jason put you in the car, and I started to drive. It's obvious that you really need to lay low for a while."

It was hard for K.Y to concentrate with the constant throbbing that was occurring in his head. Everything from his temple down to the bottom of his feet was killing him, and all he wanted to do was take a warm bath and relax. He used the little bit of strength that he had to sit up to see the damage that had been done.

He had two large bandages on his forehead, and his left eye was so swollen it was hard for him to even open it. He immediately became enraged.

"Who the fuck could have done this to me," he screamed. "Turn the fuck around. Someone is going to get it tonight!"

"Kyle, I know you're upset, and I don't blame you," Tammy said in a surprisingly calm demeanor. "Regardless of what you're feeling, you have to act rationally. Once word gets out that you've been robbed, that is exactly what everyone will be expecting you to do. It's best to leave your enemies in suspicion. That's exactly how you ended up in this situation in the first place. Everything about you is so predictable."

"How the fuck can you be so calm and relaxed after what the hell just happened to me," he shouted. "I need to find out who did this and handle them fuck niggas right now."

"Look, I know you're angry, hurt, and confused. But I can promise you that retaliating right away is only going to bring heat and trouble to the organization," Tammy replied in a warm, soft tone. "As much as I want to run up on those fools and help you get back whatever you lost, we have to focus on the bigger picture and not just this little battle."

Usually, K.Y would have taken her advice, but he was so angry and bewildered about what had just occurred. He knew that he would not rest comfortably until his enemy was feeling the same thing that he was.

"Shut the fuck up and turn this damn car around," he said with much authority as he slammed his fist on the dashboard. "Save that tranquil and peaceful shit for someone else. Take me home so I can go get my shit back from those bums," he screamed out with fire in his voice.

Tammy took the steering wheel and quickly sped through two lanes of traffic on the busy highway until she reached the breakdown lane. She parked the car and took off her seat belt.

"What the fuck is that going to solve, huh? You still got your ass whooped, and whatever shit you lost is probably fucking gone by now," she yelled back angrily. She paused, took a deep breath, lowered her voice, and then continued.

"Look, you're not going to win every mêlée you fight, but remember what is important is winning the war. That's why it's essential to choose your battles carefully and when it's important to just charge it to the game.

Have you ever heard of the serenity prayer," she asked him, changing the direction of the conversation and again softening her tone.

After a nod from Kyle, she continued.

"You got robbed. They beat your ass. You lost product, and now you're hurt. No matter how angry you get or how many times you relive that moment in your mind, you cannot change it or do it over again. The only thing that you can do is accept that it happened and appreciate the lessons you learned from this and come back stronger.

Now, if you want to go home and play inspector gadget, we can do that, or you can go enjoy this bungalow that I got for us right next to the beach. You just let me know what you want to do, boss," she said, this time adding a sexy sass to her tone.

The thought of laying up next to Tammy for a few nights caused him to reconsider his previous request to go back home.

"You always know exactly what to say to make saying no to you impossible," he said as he laid back in his seat. "I'll relax and go home on beast mode. Those niggas won't know what hit them when I make it back to Orlando," he said, meaning every word of it.

"Good," Tammy replied with a smile as she sped off and headed to the direction of their small piece of paradise.

***

He imagined the bungalow that Tammy rented would be amazing. However, he was still in complete shock when they first entered the place they would be relaxing in for the next few days.

Kyle immediately noticed the shadows of flames dancing through the cozy abode. The movement from at least a hundred candles gave off the right amount of light and warmth.

"I do have a sweet side that I don't show that often," Tammy said when she noticed his expression. "I called in a favor because I really wanted you to be able to come here, relax, and forget about everything that just happened. I hope you like it."

"I had no idea you cared this much," he joked, trying to keep everything light. "I love it, though. Thank you."

"I figured I've given you enough hell throughout the last few months. It's obvious that you can take whatever I dish out to you, so I thought it was about time I showed you the softer side to me," she said as she took his hand and led him over to the large bed in the bedroom.

"I just want you to spend the next few days relaxing, so that way when you get back, you'll be much stronger than you were before. I'm going to go to the kitchen to make us something to eat. If you look in the drawer next to you, you will find a few L's to help you relax and forget about the pain. If you need anything else just let me know."

Before she walked out of the bedroom, she slipped off the long maxi dress she had been wearing to reveal her all-black lace bra and boy shorts.

Kyle turned on the large flat screen T.V, lit the large pre-rolled blunt, and attempted to watch the news before the relaxation he finally felt caused him to fall asleep.

Kyle couldn't remember the last time he could fall into such a deep and pleasant sleep. Still, the munchies he was feeling and the delightful aromas that were swaying through his nostrils made it impossible to remain in his peaceful slumber.

He walked into the large kitchen to find Tammy setting the table for the delicious meal she had prepared for him.

"Damn, girl. I had no idea that you could cook," he said as he took his seat in front of the plate that she had arranged for him.

Tammy took her seat at the table across from him and bowed her head to pray over the meal.

Kyle couldn't wait and immediately dug into his rice, beans, and steak.

"This shit is good," he managed to say in between large mouthfuls of food. "Who the hell taught you how to cook?"

"Fool," Tammy started with a slight attitude. "Don't you ever interrupt me while I'm praying," she said, meaning every word.

"My bad. I guess you just never struck me as a religious type of person."

"I'm not religious; I'm spiritual. There is a difference. Anyway, my mother taught me to cook as soon as I was tall enough to see over the stove," she responded with a snicker. "Obviously, there is a lot of things that you don't know about me."

"It's only because you're so distant and secretive most of the time. Every time I try to get close to you, you just pull away from me."

Tammy put her fork down and took a deep breath before she responded. "You and I just come from two completely different worlds," she said softly. "You let your emotions run you, and I'm just not built like that." Tammy excused herself from the table and grabbed as many dishes as she could carry to the sink. Kyle watched her go into the cupboard and grab two wine glasses and a chilled bottle of wine from the wine cooler.

"I have a couple blankets and jackets close by the beach if you care to join," she said before she vanished outside.

Kyle quickly ate a few more bites of his food before following Tammy in the direction she had just gone in.

The cool November night was peaceful and relaxing for both Kyle and Tammy, who had both been stressed from the risks of their chosen hustle.

"Aren't you cold out here," he asked with much concern.

"I use to live in Boston, Massachusetts. I will not feel cold unless there is snow around. The breeze does feel nice, though. I really needed this," she said as she lowered herself onto the blanket that was positioned on the soft beach sand.

"Tell me about it," he replied after he followed suit and got comfortable alongside Tammy.

Kyle grabbed the other blanket that she had folded up neatly next to them and opened it to keep Tammy warm.

"You're so thoughtful sometimes," she said as she wrapped herself in the blanket and snuggled closer to him. "You will make some woman really happy one day."

"I don't want to make some random woman happy. I want that woman to be you."

"Let's be serious with each other here. I know your background, and I've heard a lot about your reputation. I'm probably one of the few women you have ever met that doesn't throw herself desperately at you. You're used to being able to select whatever woman you want, and for the first time, you realize that you don't always got it like that. I'm a challenge to you, and once you feel like you've conquered this challenge, you and I both know you'll be on to something else."

"You really think you know everything, don't you? I get it that you're older than me, and you've seen and done more, but it doesn't mean that you have the answers to everything."

"I never once implied that, but that's how you perceive my words. Yes, I have seen a lot, and I honestly feel like I've lived a million lives in the short amount of time I've been on this Earth. I've learned a lot of valuable lessons, and most of them I had to learn the hard way," she said as she sat up to open the bottle of wine.

"You and I see tons of money weekly. What means more than all of the jewelry, money, and material things that money can buy," she asked, changing the direction of their conversation.

"Love," he replied frankly.

"You can be such a hopeless romantic. That's where we are different. To me, wisdom is priceless."

"Wisdom is great, and I appreciate all that you give me, but wisdom isn't going to hold you at night or comfort you when you need it. Yeah, it's going to help you get more than you could possibly dream for, but what good is all of the gold and silver in the world if you don't have someone to share it with? What good is the fancy car or house if you don't have that special person you love to give you happy memories?"

"Most people are full of shit," she replied flatly. "Most people have their own needs to fulfill and their own motives for dealing with you. You want love, but who is to say the woman you fall in love with doesn't want something else? Love is just a weakness that makes it easier for your opponent to defeat you.

Let's not forget that no one is perfect. Can you really see yourself settling with someone's negative qualities just for the sake of not spending your life alone," she asked with much curiosity.

"That's the best part about it. I read once that 'We don't come to love by finding a perfect person, but seeing an imperfect person perfectly.' My mother taught me that you take them for their good and bad qualities when you love someone, and you don't hold it against them. You love them for who they are and not what they can do for you."

"I have to say I'm quite shocked by your response. For starters, I had no idea that you could read," Tammy laughed as she gave him a light punch on his shoulders to let him know she was just joking. "Your mom sounds like a wise woman. How come you don't talk about her much?"

"She was a wise woman, but sadly she isn't anymore. It's hard to talk about her because I hate having to remember where she and I once were to where we are now.

My mother used to be the one person I felt I could fully trust and always had my back, but then she turned on me."

"What happened," she asked.

"Drugs," he replied dismally. "My mother went from being a dedicated and loving mother who worked hard and loved harder to a street whore who would do anything for a quick fix."

"That sounds rough." Tammy reached over and softly laid her hand and her head on his chest to try to comfort him after the painful memory he just shared.

"It's crazy how you seem so optimistic about finding love and the perfect woman, but your words were so harsh when you were just speaking about your mother."

"I don't know if I will ever be able to forgive her for the shit that she put my siblings and me through. She seemed eager to find them the night they went missing, but the next day she sold their shit so she could get high. She didn't even seem to have an ounce of remorse for any of it," he said coldly.

"I'm not going to sit here and preach like I know shit about love because I don't, but I can say that I know a huge part of that is being able to forgive.

Although I'll never know the pain of what you had to endure with your mother, I have had to deal with my share of pain throughout my life also. Pain, hurt, and anger can and will consume you if you allow it to. The reason it's been so hard for you to talk about the story with your mother is because you haven't been able to let go and forgive her. I don't know what demons she had to deal with to get her to the point that she is now, and neither do you. I'm not suggesting that you forget what all she has done to you, but if you have faith in love that strong, then you have to have faith that love can and will conquer all things, right?"

"I guess so. I just don't see how she will ever turn around. She saw the shit that happened to Ra's mom when she fell deep into her addiction. Hell, she was there for him when his mom OD'd and everything. I just don't think I'll ever understand how she managed to fall so hard and so fast despite all of the shit she's seen and experienced."

"Life is not meant for you to understand it. You'll drive yourself crazy trying to figure out people and why they do the things that they do. Instead, you have to learn how to have inner peace. Being still and calm in a world so crazy and chaotic is the best gift you can possibly give yourself. Nothing you did could have caused your mother to be where she is now, but you seem to carry so much of the burden and pain on you.

Pray for her to get better, but most importantly, pray for you to find that peace to get through this storm because whether your mom beats this or not, you can't let this hold you down forever."

Kyle didn't immediately respond to her last statement. He had not cried since the night he discovered his own siblings went missing on his watch. From that moment, he had continued to blame himself for the whole downfall of his family.

"It was my fault," he said, barely audible as he tried desperately to hide the tears that were beginning to form in his eyes.

Tammy could feel the apparent change in his temperament and decided to wait patiently instead of prying further into it. She listened to the rhythm of his heart's dance get faster while his breathing seemed to get heavier with each breath.

"Crying doesn't make you weak," she said as she used her manicured hands to rub over his chest. "It's actually proof that you've been strong for too long. Sometimes you need to cleanse and get it all out; holding on to all of that only hurts you and your mental state."

The lump in his throat from holding back years of woe and guilt only seemed to grow larger and heavier as Tammy did her best to assuage him. Kyle was always taught that men were not supposed to cry. Although Tammy assured him it was ok, he was not ready to display such a soft and vulnerable side to anyone.

He spoke in a slow and soft tone to try to maintain control of his emotions.

"My mother left me in charge of my siblings while she was out whoring," he started. "I was supposed to stay home and watch them. They were so young at the time, but hell, my mom had left me alone at their age before. I thought it would be ok to just hit the block and make some money instead of staying locked up in that damn house.

I wasn't even gone that fucking long." He paused. His tears were becoming more difficult to fight as he became angrier, reliving that ghastly night. "I just got a hold of some ye' and wanted to get rid of it. I watched my mom practically sell her morals and soul for the same product that I was trying to sell to people on my own street. Ra and I dragged her home to find an empty house. When I left, they were there, sleeping soundly and peacefully in the beds that I had tucked them into."

He stopped speaking because he could no longer fight the inevitable. He succumbed to his emotions as his salty tears flowed freely down his cheeks.

"This is your fault," she kept screaming out to me. I was frozen because I was in such a state of shock. Her first few blows to my head didn't faze me because everything was numb.

Once I snapped out of it, I was so angry because I felt like it was really her fault. I threw the product I had on me to her, and I told her to go kill herself with it. I swear I didn't mean it, but if she hadn't been out chasing a high, she would have been home like she was supposed to, and none of this shit would have happened.

Keenan was like my mini-me," he said as a slight smile crept up on his face. "He wanted to be like me. He would try walking like me and talking like me. We went to basketball games, and I would cheer him on at his soccer games.

Kenya was a genius. I knew that from when that girl was really little. If there was one thing I was sure about in life, it was that she would be the one to grow up and be somebody. I knew out of all of us she would be the one to be successful and make it out of the hood; now they're both gone."

Kyle cried until his head hurt, and he had no more tears left to cry. Once Tammy heard the sound of his quickly pulsating heart return to its regular pace, she sat up and gently wiped away the tears that he had finally let go. She leaned in and gently kissed his forehead with her soft lips before returning to her comfortable position of laying her head on his chest with her arms wrapped tightly around him.

"She binged for weeks, and her newfound addiction escalated faster than anything I've ever seen. She would only come by the house when I was gone, and it was only to see what she could steal so she could sell and use the money to go get high. I tried to help her a couple times, but we always ended up fighting whenever we spoke more than a couple words to each other.

I gave up on finding my siblings and getting my mother back many years ago. Still, I've never gotten over the agony of the truth of everything that happened."

"It's not your fault Kyle. We are humans, and we make mistakes. You didn't do any of this on purpose. You can't carry this around all your life."

Kyle exhaled deeply, and for the first time since he lost his family, he actually felt a sense of relief.

Tammy pulled out an L that was in the pocket of one of the hoodies. She lit it and handed it to him.

Kyle inhaled the smoke deeply and held it for as long as he could before exhaling. He repeated this several times before the wine and weed had him even more relaxed.

"If this is what you mean by inner peace, then I really need to find that bitch now," he said.

"Kind of, but not quite," she responded. "Inner peace means that you don't need anything like a blunt or drink to give you peace and make you more relaxed and at ease with your present situation. You have to learn to trust your struggle and know that you're going through it for a reason. I remember when I used to smoke, it always put me in a 'fuck it' type of mindset. When you have that inner peace, you learn how to achieve that feeling on your own."

"I'll get it one day, but this is definitely a start for me."

***

Tammy was awakened peacefully when the small light emitting through the horizon from the early morning sun reached her eyes. She got up from the blanket they had fallen asleep on and briefly stretched before going in the house to start breakfast and a bath for Kyle.

She had just finished preparing the meal when she heard the door to the outside patio close shut.

"Thanks for last night," Kyle said before going to the bathroom to wash up for breakfast.

"I feel so much better after finally telling someone and getting this off of my chest." Once again, he took his seat in front of his plate. But this time, he bowed his head for grace once Tammy did the same.

"I'm going to get some people to move all that shit out of my mother's house as soon as we get back so your girl can move in," he said once they were done praying. "I need to get out of there and stop letting my past hold me back."

"Did you have a chance to move out all of your valuables," Tammy asked.

"Ain't shit really valuable in there besides the safe in my room. Everything else can go."

"Kyle, please tell me you don't have any real money or product inside the house that you live in right there in the middle of the hood," Tammy said with much concern.

"Where else could I put it? I don't trust anyone else to hold almost a quarter-million dollars of my life savings," he replied casually.

"Kyle, do you at least have someone house sitting or a couple of cameras in your house just in case."

Kyle's silence was enough to confirm what Tammy had already suspected.

"You have a quarter of a million dollars sitting unguarded in your house," Tammy yelled out as she almost choked on her eggs benedict.

She tried to remain calm, but the fact that he had once again proven himself to be such a novice agitated her. She spoke slowly and low to avoid giving away how annoyed she really was. "Who else knows that the money is there?"

"Ra," he responded. Without Tammy having to go off, he realized his mistake by leaving his life savings unguarded.

"Clean this fucking place up. I'm going to put everything in the car. We are out of here in the next two minutes," she said urgently.

It took less than she planned to get everything packed back in the car and get back on the road home.

"You have a quarter of a million dollars in savings in your house. What all did you lose the other night when they jumped you?"

"Ten grand and ten pounds," he replied softly.

"You don't have any other place where you store your money or product," Tammy asked.

He was hesitant to respond.

"I don't care if you're keeping it at one of your bitch's house," she stated. "Just be honest with me. I can't help you if I don't know what you've got going on, and it's obvious that with two straight days full of mistakes that you need as much help as you can get."

"I have a safe at Keisha's house. I only had twenty thousand in that safe."

"So you don't have any more product, and it's possible that you could be walking home to an empty safe. You mean to tell me that all you have on you is twenty grand that you left stashed at some broad's house?"

"That's all I got," he replied somberly.

***

"Thanks for the free cash pussy boy," scribbled on a sheet of paper is all he found in the spot where his safe use to be.

"I can't believe this shit," he screamed out. "They stole my money, my safe, and these niggas even took off with my clothes and Jordan collection. When I find out who the hell did this, I'm killing that motherfucker on site!"

Tammy sat at the edge of the bed silently; she was frozen and almost in a complete daze.

"Well," he spoke up. "Say something! This shit and your silence is driving me fucking crazy."

The sound of his thunderous voice talking broke her out of the trance that she was in.

"No need in crying over spilled milk. We need to go to Keisha's house and get everything you have over there, now," Tammy said as she stood up. "How much do you really trust that bitch anyway?"

Once again, K.Y was hesitant to answer her question.

"I don't care about who you're seeing or fucking; just answer the damn question."

"In the five years I've been fucking with her, my money or products have never come up short or gone missing."

Tammy didn't even flinch at him confirming that he was still indeed dealing with her like that.

"When you get over there, it is important that you don't treat her any differently just because I'm there. You need to be calm, cool, and collected, and try not to give her any information about what's going on."

"I don't think it's a good idea that we both go. I'll just go grab the shit and meet you back here."

"Nigga," she said with much aggravation. "You think you're going to leave me in this raggedy-ass house in the middle of the hood that just got robbed? I don't think so. Anyway, I need to peep her attitude and see where her head is. For all you know, she could be part of the problem."

"Well, I have to warn you that Keisha is one crazy bitch," Kyle responded.

"I can promise you that she isn't crazier than me."

***

They pulled up in front of Keisha's apartment building on Mercy drive and practically ran up the steps to try to get the money he had left so they could go and make moves. Once they found apartment 3D, K.Y knocked four times, loudly, on the door.

"Who da fuck dat is," a woman's voice screamed out from the other side of the door with the thickest country accent Tammy had ever heard.

"K.Y," he yelled back.

After several seconds and many unlocked locks later, Keisha flung the door open. She had her hand on her hip, wearing just a cropped tee and some frilly pink Victoria Secret boy shorts.

"Motherfucker, you got a lot of damn nerves thinking you can just go and come whenever the hell you please," she said while violently rolling her neck as she spoke. "And, who the fuck is this bitch," Keisha asked, directing her anger and aggravation towards Tammy.

"I'm K.Y's cousin. He was giving me a ride home and said that he wanted to stop by and see you while we were still on this side of town," Tammy stated with a smile.

The thought of K.Y potentially missing her like she had missed him was enough to get her to soften her tone up a little.

"Hmmm. Get in," Keisha muttered as she moved from out of the doorway to let the two of them inside.

"What da hell happened to ya face," she asked once she noticed the bandages, bruising, and swelling from K.Y's previous attack.

"I don't want to talk about it," he replied. "It's a long story. Look, I just need to grab a few things and bounce. I'll be back to check on you in a couple of days."

"Oh hell no," Keisha screamed as her anger returned. "What da fuck dis look like to you? I ain't seen yo ass in weeks, then you come up in my house with another bitch talking about she yo damn cousin just to grab yo shit and leave? If you grabbin' yo shit den, you need to grab all of it because I'm not puttin' up wit dis shit no mo! Get all yo shit and get the hell outta my damn house and my life."

Without bothering to argue with her, K.Y went to the room and grabbed a couple of duffle bags he had in her closet. One contained some of his clothes, and the other one had a few pairs of his shoes. He grabbed an empty duffle bag and proceeded to empty out the contents of his safe into the bag.

After a brief inspection to make sure that he didn't leave anything behind, he slung his bags over his shoulder and headed back out to the living room.

"Girl, I just ain't gon' do dis no mo. I hear what you sayin', but dis ain't fair to me or my kids. Kyle been doin' dis to me for years, and it's time I finally realize dat shit ain't gon' change," Kyle overheard Keisha complaining to Tammy.

"Just take a minute to calm down. Hit him up in a couple days if you change your mind. He's got a lot going on, and he's just not thinking clearly," Tammy mentioned as she tried to assuage Keisha's feelings.

By the time Kyle had returned to the living room, the once fuming Keisha was much more calm and relaxed.

"Let's go," Kyle told Tammy as he headed straight to the door.

"It's cool cuz," Tammy replied. "I'm in no rush. Give me the keys. I'll take your bags to the car and give you two a minute to talk." As they were making the exchange, Tammy gave him a very intense look.

"It was nice to finally meet you, girl," Tammy mentioned as she opened the door to leave.

"Likewise, girl, and I'm sorry for goin' off on yo ass earlier," Keisha replied with a chuckle.

***

Kyle had only spent an additional fifteen minutes upstairs before he left to join Tammy.

He hopped in the driver's side of his car, put the car in drive, and headed in the direction of his house.

"I had a feeling you couldn't last that long," she started. "But only 15 minutes?"

It took a minute for Kyle to understand the joke that she was making on him.

"First of all, I have no problem laying it down, and I definitely last more than fifteen minutes."

"Well, you sure could have fooled me. You know it's important for Keisha to not be mad at you right now. I left you up there to fix shit with her. What the hell were you doing all of that time then?"

"We talked. That's it. I told her that she was tripping and I would be back when I had more time."

"Ugh," Tammy groaned with much disgust. "Sometimes you really make me feel like I do all of this talking for no reason. You were supposed to be back in her good graces by the time you left that place. Right now, that bitch is probably fuming in her apartment, and trust me, there is nothing worse than a woman scorned. You can't afford to have one of those right now."

"I'm not in the mood to hear this shit," he responded dismally. "I would really appreciate it if you would just stop talking."

"Excuse me?"

"I got my ass whooped, I've lost ten pounds of product, and over a quarter of a million dollars in two fucking days. I don't want to hear the woman I love and want to be with encourage me to go fix issues with the next bitch. So could you please just shut yo' ass up?"

Tammy didn't respond. Not only was she shocked to hear him open up about his feelings about her, but she was also surprised he had spoken to her with so much authority.

"What the hell is it going to take to get you to understand that I don't want to be with anyone else but you? All I want is for you to stop being so damn stubborn and let me in. We've been doing this dance for months, and I never seem to get close enough to you."

"Kyle," Tammy started. "You've been trying hard for months, but at the same time, it's evident that you couldn't have been that serious about me because you were still doing you. I'm not mad because I can't be. You're not my man, and I can't be pissed off about it. You're a man, and you have needs.

However, how do you expect me to believe anything that you're saying when you're still doing you?"

"You've been playing games, Tee. I want nothing more than for shit to get serious and take us to the next level. If you gave me a real shot, you wouldn't have to worry about any of these bitches, and I can put that on everything I've ever loved. I'm seriously trying to build a relationship with you."

"Fuck a relationship," Tammy stated bluntly. "I'm about building an empire." She paused a moment before she softened her tone and continued. "You don't know anything about me, my past, or why I am the way that I am. I never saw two people really love each other. My parent's relationship was so fucked up that I really don't like to ever talk about it.

My mom and pops didn't even speak that often and when they did, it was a huge showdown. Hell, they didn't even like each other enough to sleep on the same side of the house, much less the same bed. They stayed together because they thought it was the best for my siblings and me, which couldn't be any further from the truth. People are supposed to learn about love and trust from home and the shit they see their parents do, but I never learned that.

My mother couldn't trust that motherfucker further than she could throw him, which wasn't far because my mother is very frail," she tittered. "I was eleven the first time she coached me on what she wanted me to ask him during one of our many conversations. She attached a wire to me to record the whole thing. To be honest, I'm more interested in trying to catch someone in a lie than to really believe anything that comes out of their mouth now.

I hear everything you say to me, but I guess I'm really just someone who needs to see it and not just hear it. You talk a really good talk, but I need to see you back it up if you really mean what you say."

"I'm willing to do whatever so that we can grow."

"I'll be willing to give you a benefit of the doubt," she said. "But only under one condition."

"Name it."

"I need you to finally admit that you don't know what the hell you're doing. You also have to give me permission to do what is necessary to take your business to the next level. I need to know that you're going to stop being so stubborn and do all that it takes to get you back on your feet again."

He sighed deeply before responding. "It's beyond obvious that I'm not as good as I once thought I was. Clearly, I need your help to start my business again, but this time I want to do it the right way. I won't fight you on anything anymore."

"Then let's build this empire."

CHAPTER TEN

"So you're really not going to let me get a key," Kyle asked Tammy for what felt like the millionth time.

"I don't know why you keep asking me like my answer is going to change. I said no before, and you will continue to get no as the answer. You should count your blessings that I even allow you to stay here," Tammy stated as she unlocked the door to the apartment. "You don't pay any rent or bills here, and you have been able to come and go as you please for the last four months now."

They walked into the spacious two-bedroom apartment, and she placed her keys on the key hook next to the door.

"It's not the same Tee, and you know it. If the problem is me not paying rent, then I'll pay all the bills in here, but I'm tired of having to call you and have you meet me whenever I'm trying to get my stuff that's here in the house."

"I've had a long day, and I'm really not in the mood to argue with you or hear you bitch about foolishness. I'm allowing you to save some money so that you can get back on your feet, but if you don't like the arrangement as it is now, then you are more than welcome to leave whenever you are ready to."

"Of course, that isn't what I want to do, but it just sucks feeling like I don't have a house of my own anymore. I moved out of my old spot because you thought it was best, and now I don't have any place to call home."

"What do you expect Kyle," she asked as she washed her hands to prepare their dinner for the evening. "I told you that you should go and get a place of your own, but you don't want that, and I don't blame you. It's stupid to keep your shit where you will be sleeping, and you

103

don't want to try to work things out with Keisha so you can store stuff at her place. And you know good and damn well I'm not letting you keep a thing over here. You still don't know who robbed you for sure, and I am really putting my reputation and safety at risk to allow you to even be here so often. Not to mention, my pops would kill me if he found out I was shacking up with a man, much less someone that I wasn't even married to. It's like all you can think about here is yourself. You really need to stop being so selfish."

Kyle reached into his pocket without saying another word, pulled out a baby blue Tiffany's box, and sat it on the counter next to where Tammy was standing.

"Kyle, what is that," she inquired as a smile crept up on her face.

"Open it."

Tammy's eyes grew wide in surprise as she opened the box to see a 2.5 carat Tiffany Embrace ring sitting inside of the box.

"Kyle," Tammy exclaimed. "This is a $50,000 ring! How the hell were you able to afford this?"

K.Y was surprised at her knowledge of the expensive engagement ring he had purchased for her.

"I'm tired of just telling you I want you to be mine," he responded. "I'm showing you that this is how it needs to be.

No woman has ever made me feel the way you do, and that ring is my way of promising you that I will do whatever it takes to make you happy. You deserve it all, and I just want to be the one to give it to you."

Tammy stared longingly at the stunning and flawless diamond ring she had just received. "It's beautiful," she whispered.

"You're beautiful," he replied back. "You're smart, classy, sassy, spiritual, and because of you, I'm pushing myself higher than I ever thought possible. In the beginning, I hated the way you treated me because you were such a challenge and a pain in my ass," he chuckled.

"But all of it was to turn me into the man I am becoming today, all because you believed in me enough to push me and help me do more. Now that I've had you in my life, I don't want to imagine living it without you next to me."

In the ten months K.Y had been dealing with Tammy, he rarely saw any kind of real emotions out of her. During the four months that they had been living together, their bond became much closer. And she slowly allowed him to learn more and more about her.

She shared more stories about her childhood and her messed-up views of love and relationships due to her parents' vehement relationship. She also clarified the man she addressed as pops was actually her stepdad. Because her mother had two failed marriages, she couldn't imagine having one of her own.

"Most little girls dream of one day growing up and becoming a beautiful bride, but I don't think I'll ever get married," she shared to him one night during one of their late-night conversations.

"My mom married my pops, not for love, but instead for the stability that he provided.

Since it was two people who were simply tolerating each other instead of two people loving each other, they rarely got along. She was unhappy, and it would show in the way that she treated us sometimes. I don't know if it was because her parents weren't around or if it was because of my pops, but I can count on my hands how many times my mother actually told me she loved me. We never hugged me, and when the rare occasion came when she did want to touch me, it just felt weird because I wasn't use to that kind of affection at all.

I try not to complain about it because I really did have it all growing up. My mom made some pretty big sacrifices for us to live good, but I don't think I could ever do that. He was hardly ever home, and when he was there, it was like World War 3. He didn't talk to my mother like the queen she is, and it didn't help that my mother knew about the array of women he was dealing with.

I think what hurt the most wasn't even seeing them physically fighting or even the mental abuse that was constantly going on between them. But it was having to spend every day of my life pretending that everything was ok. I still had to smile for every family portrait, attend every family reunion, party, cookout, and everything else in between. I had to do it while putting on this big ass front that we were one happy family. I hated that more than anything. I think maybe that's why I'm so blunt with my thoughts and feelings now," she said with a wink to acknowledge how rude she sometimes came off.

All of the conversations they had about marriage, love, relationships, and family made K.Y incredibly nervous and hesitant to express his desire to have her in his life forever. Tammy's motto, however, had always been, "Any questions that you don't ask will always have a 'no' answer."

"Will you do me the honor of being my wife," he asked her, finally breaking their silence.

Tammy took a deep breath and hung her head down low, so low that her large curls covered her face and made it impossible for K.Y to read her facial expressions.

"I don't know what to say," the usually outspoken and super confident Tammy replied timidly.

"I'm cool with not getting an answer now," K.Y responded as he placed his arms around her and used his hands to raise her head. Once their eyes met, he continued speaking.

"I had a feeling that you wouldn't be ready for something like this, and all I want you to do is promise me that you'll think about it."

"I promise," she replied with a smile.

***

Ned's was unsurprisingly packed when Tammy and K.Y arrived. Although she didn't give him the answer he had hoped for, K.Y still wanted to celebrate.

"I should have listened to you a long time ago," K.Y said after taking a large sip of his beer.

"I'm just glad I finally got through your thick skull," she laughed. "I give you a hard time, but you're smarter than I give you credit. Sometimes I really do forget that you're only 23. I don't think I've ever met someone your age with as much dedication and ambition. It's admirable."

"Thank you," K.Y replied. "That really means a lot, especially coming from you. Now, thanks to you, I finally got back all the money from those that owed me, and I have a few people out handling my runs for me also," he said. "I like enjoying a nice dinner with you like old times while I got other people out there making my money."

"I've been trying to tell you that, but you didn't want to listen in the beginning. I'm happy that you're happy now. I was getting tired of having to bitch at you all the damn time," Tammy chuckled.

The rest of the evening flowed with smiles, jokes, and laughter between the two of them. Neither one of them seemed to want the night to be over.

Instead of just heading back to Tammy's apartment, they decided to go walk around the lake directly behind the restaurant. That way, they could burn off some of the calories they had just consumed.

The evening was just perfect for a stroll around the lake, reflecting back the beautiful light the stars above were radiating. After walking a few laps, they walked over to a nearby park and sat next to each other on the swings.

"Kyle, you've got a flock of girls that would love to be Mrs. Cole. Why don't you go and marry one of them?"

He was completely thrown off by what she said because everything about the night seemed to be going great.

"You're still so young and have so much more living and growing to do. You are supposed to be enjoying your selfish years. You're supposed to travel the world and see how many businesses you can build, not trying to marry a woman six years older than you."

"I would be a fool to let someone like you just walk out of my life. I've always had a flock of women chasing my money and what I could do for them. I've never really had anyone around me who didn't care about that other shit and just cared about me as a person.

I'm going to travel the world, but I want to share those memories with you. I am going to build as many businesses as I can, but I want you there as my partner for everything."

"What's wrong with how things are now," she retorted. "I'm here when you need me, and I have never and will never let you down. To me, titles just mess up good things because there are just way too many expectations that come with it.

Why can't we just be Tammy and Kyle? Why do we have to complicate it with anything else?"

"How is telling the world how much I love you and want you going to complicate anything? I want to show those around me, but most importantly your family and God, that I'm going to do whatever I need to in order to make sure you are protected, safe, and well taken care of at all times. You said you wanted action, and I'm taking that step in showing you how serious I am about keeping you in my life."

"This is all just so new, Kyle. I've never had anyone show me love the way that you do before.

I love my old man more than life, but the way he reciprocates it is different from this. He shows me love by making sure I have the knowledge I need to not let someone take advantage of me or taking care of the financial things I need. I never really realized how good it would feel to have something like this in my life too. He has always been a very realistic person and would always tell me that if something seems too good to be true, then it is. Something about you makes me want to believe what you say."

"You should," he said as he grabbed her hand and interlocked her fingers with his.

"I'm not putting a rush on you to make a decision. The ring is yours to do with it whatever you want. If you want to wear it cool, or if you want to put it up and think about it more, I'm cool with that too. I just want you to seriously consider my proposal. You're worth so much more than the love you've been given."

Even though the park was dimly lit, it still could not hide the smile that his words brought to her face. Kyle got up from his seat on the swing and helped her up. He pulled her close to him and did something that he wanted to do the moment he met her. He gently kissed her lips, and to his surprise, she didn't fight and was not reluctant like she had been in the past. Instead, she placed her two hands gently on the sides of his face and returned the sweet love and affection he had shown to her.

***

Their night together had been amazing. Kyle had finally shared a real intimate moment with Tammy, and he couldn't wait to make it back to the apartment with hopes of turning that kiss into much more.

"Didn't you lock the door," Tammy asked Kyle as she reached the top of the stairs.

"I don't have a key remember? You locked the door like you always do."

"Well, it's not locked now," she whispered.

Kyle removed his pistol from his hip. "Go wait for me in the car. I'll check everything out to make sure it's good," he demanded.

"Hell no," Tammy responded. "I can't let you go in there by yourself. I'm coming too." She reached into her purse and pulled out her 9mm.

"You have a gun," he asked, surprised to see her pull out her own protection.

"What," she questioned. "You thought I only know how to pack washers and dryers? I always carry protection, and I know how to use it also."

Kyle stood there for a moment, confused about what to do next. Although he found it very attractive to see Tammy holding her gun, willing to have his back no matter what, he couldn't risk anything happening to her.

"I got this," he said as he tried to assure her that it would be okay to enter the apartment alone. "I really would prefer for you to just wait for me downstairs."

"You have two options. You can either lead or be led. Which position do you want," Tammy asked as she put one in the head of the gun. "I can't and won't let you go in there by yourself."

Since her mind was made up, he knew that there was no way to try to convince her to do otherwise. He opened the door and quietly walked into the apartment.

"You already know who it is motherfuckers," Tammy screamed out once she was inside. "Come out now with your hands up, and I might let you leave with your life."

Kyle tried to shush her as quickly and quietly as he could, but he knew it was too late. If anyone was still in the house, they had just lost their element of surprise.

"Don't shush me," she snapped at him. "Niggas know not to fuck with me, so I'm not sure why anyone would have pulled a move like this on me."

He sauntered throughout the rooms of the house, just in case that the intruder was still present. He kept his protection ready to fire in case he made his presence known. They made it to the last bedroom, their bedroom, and still had not seen anyone on the premises.

"It's clear," Kyle said as he entered the bathroom. "It's weird. Besides this note on the mirror, everything else still looks like it's in its place."

She walked into the large bathroom in her room and dropped to the floor, crying loudly from her devastation.

Before they left for dinner, Tammy placed the ring Kyle gave her on the counter next to all of her jewelry. Instead of finding the ring where she had left it, she noticed the box was empty and a note scribbled in the same handwriting in the last letter they found read, "HA! NOT FUCKING HAPPENING!"

CHAPTER ELEVEN

"I'll just buy you a new one," K.Y declared as he tried to comfort Tammy. "Look at it this way, nothing else seems to be missing, and no one got hurt. It's going to be OK."

"No, it's not," Tammy bellowed in between sobs. "It's not going to be OK, and it's going to be almost impossible to fix this."

Kyle had never seen Tammy so emotional and vulnerable. He would often joke about how he thought she never knew any other emotions besides anger and happiness. He had no idea what to do or say to comfort her when she clearly needed it. He knelt down on the cold bathroom floor beside her and gently placed his arms around her.

"Don't," she said as she pulled herself away from him. "Please just leave me alone!"

Kyle knew when it was best to just let her have her way, and this was definitely one of those moments.

He closed the door behind him as he walked out to leave Tammy alone and went outside to smoke a blunt. It bothered Kyle to see her so visibly hurt. Now, he wanted more than ever to find and handle whoever was responsible for all the losses he was taking. He was finally tired of just charging everything to the game.

He pulled out his iPhone and dialed the number to the one person he had always considered his ace. The man he thought would be his friend forever and boy for life.

"What up, bruh," Rashard yelled over all the background noise. "I ain't heard from yo' ass in a minute."

"Yeah man, I just been busy taking care of some minor things. I ain't forget about you though, cuh. Anyway, you do know a phone works both ways and you haven't hit me up either. It has been a minute since we last chilled and let loose. What you got goin' on tonight," K.Y asked.

"Shit," Rashard said enthusiastically. "Just these hoes, bottles, and this hotel party that I'm throwing for one of my boys. If you ain't doing shit, you should slide through and check it out."

"Just let me know where you at, and I'll be on my way."

***

Kyle arrived at the Grand Bohemian Hotel in Orlando in less than thirty minutes. As soon as he got there, he was greeted in the lobby by a gorgeous Latina.

"Damn, papi," she said. She gently grabbed K.Y's hand as he tried to walk past her to the front counter. "You look way better in person than you do in your pictures."

Her accent was sexy, her face was beautiful, and her ass was fat. She was precisely K.Y's type. She had long, dark black, curly hair and wore a short fire red bandage dress with some leopard red bottoms. She was bad, but Kyle was no fool.

This motherfucker thinks I'm really dumb, Kyle thought to himself. *He really thought he was going to get me slippin' and off of my game with this fine ass bitch. I'm obviously going to have to remind him of who the fuck he is actually dealin' with.*

"What up, beautiful? Where is the party?"

"It's upstairs. King got us up in the Jacuzzi suite. I hope you brought your bathing suit cause I'm sure you look even better underneath those clothes."

"King," K.Y asked, clearly confused. "I don't know who that is, but I'm here to see Ra."

The woman tittered at K.Y's lack of knowledge of his friend's new nickname, "Nobody calls him that anymore loco. We all just call him King now."

Who the fuck does this nigga think he is, K.Y asked himself. *He has never and will never be shit. He only ever had a damn thing because of me and the help that I gave him.*

"Damn! I guess it's now obvious that I haven't checked for my boy in a while. I didn't know he was doing it this big now. This nigga went and got Hollywood on me," he said with a chuckle.

"Well, that's a shame, but hopefully, now that you're coming around, you keep bringing your ass around," she replied with a wink.

Out of nowhere, K.Y got a very robust urge in his stomach that

111

something just wasn't right. The nice hotel, the new nickname, the fly girl, and the fact that if he wasn't a changed man, he would have had this girl in their own room having fun in their own personal private party made him want to question everything about the situation.

In the time K.Y had been dealing with Tammy, he had seen her manipulate people to do and say exactly what she wanted them to do. He found it abnormally humorous at her ability to make others around her like her very own little marionettes, but he admired her knowledge and hustle more because of it.

How the fuck I know this bitch ain't this nigga's girl just trying to set me up or feel me out first, he asked himself. *Why else would he send someone that looks this good down here to wait for me? Why wouldn't he have just had me meet him at the room like we've always done? Why would he want me distracted with this hoes beauty before I got upstairs?*

"You look like you need a drink," she said, distracting him from his head full of thoughts as she handed him the red solo cup she had been holding. She took her manicured hand and rubbed his now tense shoulders. "I take that back. You need a few drinks and a blunt ASAP," she laughed. "You really should just try to loosen up a little."

"That does sound good. I've had a hectic day, so all I want to do now is relax. What all do y'all got up there to drink anyway," he asked as he watched her press the button to send for the elevator.

"What don't we have to drink up there is a better question. It's all top-shelf shit, and King made sure to bring out some of his expensive bottles too."

For the rest of the elevator ride, they both remained completely silent until they reached their designated floor.

"Once you've had a few more drinks and you're a little bit more relaxed, you should come look for me. Don't leave here without checking for me first," she said seductively before she sashayed away from him to join her girls.

He walked into the party, and all he saw was beer, blunts, bitches in bikinis, and expensive bottles of alcohol. Typically, K.Y would have been eager to grab him a cutie and get her to roll his blunt and make him a drink. But Tammy had put him on game at the last party she took him to.

Tammy would typically go in and mingle with those that she sold to. "It's important to know your customers," she told him before they entered the party she had previously invited him to. "You find out what they like, what they don't like, and most importantly if you should even be doing any kind of business with them. As much as I love money, I've learned that all money is damn sure not good money."

That was the same night that K.Y had seen Tammy intoxicated for the first time. Before they left for the party, she had explained that he was not allowed to drink because she would be having all the fun that night. Even though she was drunk, she could handle her liquor very well, but she couldn't stop talking and giving him guidance.

"If you don't listen to any other advice that I give you, then you need to listen to this," she slurred before each suggestion that she gave him. "Stop smoking after your bum-ass friends. Those fools put their mouths anywhere and on anybody. Then, your ass is swapping saliva with them on the same fucking blunt. Oh," she exclaimed as she thought of something else to say. "Never smoke no shit you didn't roll or see rolled, and make your own fucking drinks cause motherfuckers are sneaky as shit. They can get you fucked up and not thinking straight – or worse!"

Her advice echoed through his head, causing him to feel light-headed and out of place. Usually, Kyle was the life of the party at every party he attended. He always enjoyed getting fucked up with his boys and then end the night by fucking some girl and her friends, but now it was different. He wasn't sure if being around Tammy caused him to just become paranoid or if he was finally smart enough to see behind the fake façade that others put off. Before, he used to feel untouchable around his boys. Now, he didn't know who really had his back.

"K.Y," Ra yelled out when he finally saw his friend. "Welcome to the party, man. I'm glad you hit me up and came through. Whenever you get thirsty, or you need anything for the night, just make sure to holla at Isabella." He said as he pointed in the direction of the woman that had just met K.Y downstairs in the lobby.

"She already knows what's up. She'll get you all of your drinks, weed, and any other entertainment you need for the night. If you need anything at all, she got you."

K.Y was shocked to see that his boy was now living like this. He had always hoped that one day his friend would wake up and realize that there was more to life than the cheap clothes and raggedy cars that he was accustomed to driving. Still, he never imagined seeing him like this. Designer clothes, fancy hotel parties with expensive bottles of alcohol, and some of the baddest women that K.Y had ever seen were in attendance and anxious to spend time with Ra.

If he had any doubts before, everything that he witnessed proved the very thing that he wanted so desperately not to believe. Ra, the man that he considered and grew to love like his very own brother, had set him up for his own come up.

***

K.Y only mingled with his frenemies for a couple of hours. The stench of betrayal disgusted him and made him sick to even pretend to be around him anymore. He found everything even more peculiar that Isabella almost refused to let him leave. She tried dancing for him and getting him drunk with her strong ass drinks. When she realized none of those tricks were working, she even tried getting him to fuck her.

"I got a room a few floors down," she whispered in his ear while she gyrated her hips in his lap. She placed her large breast in his face as she leaned in again. "I normally don't do this, but you're so sexy that I just have to have you."

K.Y had made himself a couple of drinks, but he wasn't drunk or even intoxicated enough to believe the shit coming out of her mouth.

"These hoes are still using these tired ass lines," Tammy said one night during one of their conversations. "I usually don't do this. This is my first time, or I'll try it just for you," she squealed in a high pitch voice, clearly making fun of the woman who played themselves using those lines with every man they met.

"If it's a broad's first time doing something, you're going to know, and she won't have to explain shit. Nowadays, these hoes are ashamed of who they are and what they are and won't just own the fact that they do it for anyone with a cute face or fat bank account. Those types of females are used to getting attention. If they don't get it voluntarily, then they will do anything to demand it."

"Well, I respect you too much to do anything like that with you," K.Y lied as he gently tried to get her off of him. "I'd love to get to know you first before because I would hate for you to think that I'm only trying to take advantage of you."

After a few more lies, she finally got the hint. She was mad, and K.Y could tell, but he knew that if he was going to find out the truth about Ra, he had to be patient and play it cool.

He was going to do whatever it took to get the truth, and he knew he would be able to do it through Isabella.

***

"I need a vacation. I'll call you when I'm ready," was the note he found taped to the apartment door when he returned to the place he shared with Tammy.

What the hell am I going to do now, Kyle thought.

All of his clothes and shoes were stuck inside of an apartment that he had absolutely no access to. With no other choice, he got back into his car and headed to Mercy Drive to see the one person who he knew would be there for him even when he didn't always treat her right.

***

"What do you want now Kyle," Keisha asked with pure attitude in her voice from the other side of her locked apartment door.

"Can you just please open the door? I don't need or want your neighbor's nosey asses all up in our business."

"Give me one good reason why I should open the door, much less be standing here talking to you at almost three o'clock in the damn morning?"

"Cause you love and miss me," K.Y said in a sweet voice, hoping to charm her like he had always done in the past.

"Wrong answer," she replied nastily. "That's not going to work no more, Kyle. It's obvious that you're clearly taking advantage of the feelings that I have for you. You know I care about you, and that is exactly why you do me the way you do me.

Now you better say what the hell you want before I just go back in my room and take my ass back to sleep."

"I brought a couple movies, and you're favorite bottle of wine. We can watch some movies and relax like we use to," Kyle suggested.

The other side of the door was silent. He knocked again, and this time he didn't get an answer.

"Damn! Maybe I finally pissed her off enough to get her to cut me off for good," K.Y thought to himself. He never thought he would see the day when Keisha Johnson didn't want to deal with him anymore.

K.Y and Keisha were cool ever since they were in middle school, but their friendship didn't turn into more until she finally made the first move when they were both seventeen.

"When you gon' get tired of dealin' wit' dese' fast ass hoes and get you a real woman," she bluntly asked him in between breaths during their weekly basketball pickup game.

"When I find one that I actually like," he responded as he drove past her usually tight defense to score a layup. After he got the ball back, he threw it to her to check it in.

"I'm not playin' no mo' 'til you answer my question. For real, you know I like you, but you be runnin' 'round here with these fast ass, dirty foot hoes that only care about yo' dick and the money in yo' pocket. You working hard to impress bitches that ain't got shit, but you don't wanna fuck wit me, and you know I like yo' raggedy ass."

Kyle had always liked Keisha's confidence and take no bullshit kind of attitude, but sometimes she didn't know when to just be a lady.

"You talk to me like you are one of my niggas, but you expect me to want to make you my girl? Don't no man want to be with a woman with more bass in her voice than him. Now, check the ball in and finish getting' this ass whoopin.'"

Even though she never told him, she felt embarrassed at his harsh reasoning for why he never tried to pursue anything with her. After that, she started dressing more femininely and would only curse him out when he seriously pissed her off.

Despite all of that, he still didn't come on to her the way she wanted him to. Regardless, they would still have sex whenever K.Y was in the mood.

She was 19 the first time she made up her mind to just leave him alone and try to move on with her life. Her first time having sex with a man other than K.Y, she let him talk her into just sticking the head in without a condom. Nine months later, she found herself a single mom to two twin boys from a man who a coward. In fact, he decided to move back to his home country instead of helping her or paying child support.

Being the man that he was, K.Y would help Keisha when she needed it because she would let him keep some of his shit in her apartment for him.

Kyle softly knocked on the door one last time, and this time Keisha quickly unlocked the door.

"Stop making all that noise and bring yo' ass in dis' house," she said as she moved to the side to let him in.

Although she was very unwelcoming initially, it didn't take long for her to just be happy that he was there spending time with her. They watched a few movies, and she brought him up to speed with how the kids were doing until they both passed out in front of her T.V.

The sun was just rising when K.Y was awakened with a phone call from Tammy. He gently pried himself free from Keisha's grip around his chest and quietly went outside to take her call.

"Let me guess," Tammy started. "You're at Keisha's house right," she asked.

"Yeah, I am, but -," Kyle began to say before Tammy abruptly cut him off.

"It's cool. I don't care," she replied nonchalantly. "In fact, you need to stop treating that girl the way you have been. You shit on her for months and then run back whenever you need her. It's fucked up."

"How can you say that when you know I want to be with you? I'm only here to respect the space you asked for."

"How can you sleep so peacefully in the woman's house knowing that as soon as I come home, you're going to turn right back around and act like she didn't hold you down when you needed her the most? It actually helps me to prove my point that you're selfish as hell, and you only care about yourself.

Anyway, I really didn't call to argue with you. That ring wasn't the only thing that went missing that night. I didn't notice it until I watched the surveillance video.

"Video," K.Y asked, clearly confused. "You had cameras in your house? Where were they?"

"Of course I did and where they were is neither here nor there, and it certainly isn't any of your concern. I just want you to know that I know you brought work home to the crib that night. I saw you scale it and stick it in my closet. Didn't I specifically tell you not to do that? It's no wonder that someone broke in. What all did you lose last night?"

"Fifteen," he replied, letting her know he lost 15 pounds of weed.

"Do I sound like anyone who is in the mood to be playing games with you? Cut the bullshit and tell me how much of the other shit you had on you too," she said frankly.

K.Y was hesitant to answer because he knew she would be pissed off with the whole truth.

"I'm just trying to get back on my feet. I wasn't trying to - ."

"Why do you always seem to do this when I'm agitated? I'm not in the mood to hear your foolishness? Just answer the damn question," she fired back.

"Five," he replied bleakly, confessing to the five kilos of cocaine that was stashed in her closet.

"Ha," she yelled out angrily. "To think I was so hurt and upset because, for some strange reason, I blamed myself. I really believed for a moment that all of this was my fault. It's like you'll never learn, Kyle.

Every time I let my guard down for you, you just have to do something to fuck it up. You remind me every time I try to get close to you exactly why I am the way that I am and why I'll probably always be this way.

The fact that you took so much of a loss and didn't even utter a word tells me that what you lost is baby weight to what you actually have. You don't think I haven't realized that you've been keeping secrets from me? Did you really think I was that stupid? Now, you're going behind my back and deliberately doing sneaky shit that I specifically asked you not to. You brought danger to the place that I lay my head at night, and you expect me to want to marry you?

I'm going to say this, and I'm going to say it one time only, so you better listen up. You better tighten the fuck up or forget that you ever fucking met me."

With that, she ended the call and left K.Y with nothing to say because he knew that everything she had just said was true.

***

It had been two months since K.Y had last seen Tammy, and he was missing her like crazy. Keisha had taken him in and given him a key, but he missed everything from Tammy's smile and their late-night conversations to all of the delicious meals that she used to make for him.

However, this time around, he didn't just sit around, moping and put in more hours and worked extra hard. He wanted Tammy to come back. And this time, he was prepared to do things differently.

She stopped answering his calls and even disconnected the iPhone that he had purchased for her. All of her e-mails came back undeliverable, and the flowers he had delivered to her job were even refused. For the first time since they met, he had really begun to worry that she might have been completely done with him for good. The fear of losing her forever only motivated him more than ever to be successful.

"I was in Lita's shop getting my hair did when some bitch told me you be dealin' wit' some Spanish hoe named Isabella. What da fuck ya'll got goin' on," Keisha asked him boldly one night over dinner.

Kyle sucked his teeth before he finally decided to answer her question. "First of all, you've got your priorities really messed up. Weren't you just complaining to me about not having money to pay for all of your bills? Why the hell were you getting your hair done and gossiping with those other broads who don't have anything else going for themselves? All they live for is to sit around gossiping about other people."

Keisha went to cut him off, but K.Y was not in a good mood and wanted to make sure she knew he was not going to tolerate her shit.

"Don't you dare try to cut me off," he said sternly.

He paused for a moment to let his words sink in, and then he continued speaking. "Second of all, why do you always have to talk like this in front of the kids? You're way too cute to talk the way you do, and it's even more disgusting and demeaning that you do it in front of the boys. Why don't you try having some class and carrying yourself like the woman I know you can be for a change. Don't you ever get tired of just acting like some illiterate hood rat?" He threw his fork down on his plate. "Thanks a lot. You've completely ruined my appetite," Kyle spit out as he removed himself from the dinner table.

He grabbed his keys that had been hanging on the key hook next to the door, his phone, and a hefty black bag that he had by the front door and left.

***

He pulled up in front of the Grand Bohemian Hotel and once again met Isabella inside the lobby.

"Buenos noches, papi. It took you long enough to get here. I almost thought you weren't going to show."

"Nothing was going to keep me from coming to see you tonight," he said as he gently kissed her cheek and pulled her in close to embrace her.

As always, everything about Isabella was on point. From the nail polish on her toes to the curls on her head, she was always dressed to kill. He had been spending almost every night with Isabella for the last two months so he could try to get close enough to her to see what she knew about Ra. They went on many dates, and K.Y. had used a few of his connects to get him some good gifts for low prices. While she thought he was dropping a lot of money on her, it still bugged her that K.Y had not even kissed her yet.

"I got the stuff you told me to get," she said as she held the bag full of snacks and food to get them through the rest of the evening. "I also got us a couple of movies since you don't seem to be into getting any pussy," she stated sarcastically.

"It's not that. I just want to show you the respect you deserve."

They started making their way to the elevator when K.Y noticed a call coming in to his iPhone from a blocked number. He quickly told her to take the stuff upstairs and that he would join her soon before he stepped to the side to take his phone call.

"Miss me yet," the familiar voice he had longed to hear asked playfully through the phone.

"You know I do, and that's exactly why you keep pulling these disappearing acts on me. How have you been? Are you ok?"

"I've been better, but I didn't call to talk about me. I ran into your friend King," she said with a chuckle. "That fool is making so much money now that I guess he has no idea what to do with his newfound wealth, huh? I guess he never learned the lesson about trying to be inconspicuous in this game."

"Yeah, but I'm about to bring him out of his little dream world much sooner than later," K.Y replied confidently. "He clearly needs to be reminded of who the fuck I am and why he better be careful in how he deals with me."

"That's cute. I go away for a couple of months, and you grow a new, larger set of cojones. I must admit that it's rather sexy. Maybe I should take personal vacations more often if this is the reward I look forward to when I return."

"No," he replied sternly. "You need to bring your ass home. I miss you, and you made your point. No more bullshit. I'm done keeping secrets from you."

"I'm glad you said that cause I was dying to know more about this Isabella chick he told me about. She's cute."

"It's a really long story. I would much rather go over it in person," he said coyly, not wanting to admit that he just really wanted to see her again soon.

"Give me the cliff notes version, and if it seems interesting enough, then I will consider meeting up with you in person."

K.Y quickly explained how he met Isabella and the plans he had to get her to help him get his stuff back from his old friend.

"Well, it's about time you used that big ass head of yours," she laughed. "I was beginning to worry that it was only a prop for your shoulders. Meet me at Ned's tomorrow at 8:00 PM sharp, so we can get this plan moving."

***

"Why won't you fuck me," Isabella hissed after another night of just lying in the plush hotel bed watching movies with K.Y.

"Because I don't feel like it," he replied casually, never removing his eyes from the T.V screen.

"Oh, I know," she started angrily. "Your dick is little as hell, and you don't know how to use it right. That just has to be it. You're probably a minute man, and you don't know how to fuck." She got up from the bed and paraded in the red lace lingerie she had been wearing. She stood in front of the T.V and stared directly at K.Y as she spoke.

"Just admit that you couldn't handle a woman like me, so you don't want to play yourself. I just want to see what you feel like. I won't clown you in front of your boys for having the endurance of a baby," she said, this time, doubling over in laughter.

K.Y was not fazed by her stupid comments, and instead, he just shrugged his shoulders and replied," You can think whatever is going to make you feel better about me not fucking you. Now, can you please move your ass out of the way and shut the fuck up. The movie is getting good, and I would like to enjoy it in peace."

"What the fuck," she screeched out while getting in his face. "Fuck this movie, fuck these fake ass dates, gifts, and fucking flowers. Fuck going to sleep naked next to you every night and FUCK YOU," she screamed venomously with her finger all in his face. She had no idea, but K.Y had finally gotten her right where he wanted her to be.

Tammy had once proven to him during an argument that an angry tongue is as honest as a drunken one. He planned to use her emotions to his ful advantage.

He didn't match her angry demeanor, and he very calmly asked, "Would you rather me treat you like the cheap whore that King treats you like? Don't you like the fancy gifts and nice dinner dates that I take you on because you deserve stuff like that? Don't you enjoy being treated like the queen you are instead of an object just used for sex?"

"King fucks me great, unlike you," she yelled back, confirming what K.Y had already suspected. "The other shit is cool, but I just want to be sexed and touched. That motherfucker won't even look at me now that he knows I've been kicking it with you. That jealous son of a bitch won't even fuck me now, and your ass ain't doing shit either. I'm a woman, and I have needs, damn it!"

She sat on his chest and put her legs on both sides of him. She put her large breast in his face and started speaking seductively in her thick Spanish accent. "Fuck me, ahora papi. You can do whatever you want to me, but I just want you inside of me now."

K.Y was beginning to have enough. He flipped her over. K.Y could not deny or hide the fact that she was beautiful and attractive. She easily turned him on, regardless of anything else.

She saw the imprint of his large, hard member through his gray sweatpants and was instantly more turned on than she had been moments ago.

"Yeah, baby," she purred underneath him. "Give it to me just like this."

"Is this what you want," he asked sensually as he pulled her hair. She opened her legs wide so that her warm center could feel his hard penis. He lowered himself on her gently and softly kissed her breast and then her neck. He continued kissing, licking, and sucking until he reached her ear.

"I want you just as bad as you want me, but to get it, you're going to have to earn it. Are you willing to do that mami," Kyle whispered in her ear as he got a strange feeling of déjà vu.

"Yes, daddy," she said as she squirmed underneath him. "I'll do whatever you want me to."

CHAPTER TWELVE

"Well, these two months have surely been good to you," Tammy stated as she admired K.Y's physique as he took his seat at their usual table at Ned's. "You look like you've been living at the gym."

"I hate you," K.Y said bluntly as he adjusted himself in his seat.

"Ouch," Tammy pretended to be offended by his harsh word choice. "I missed you too, dear," she replied sarcastically with a wink.

"Well, don't you care to know why I feel this way?"

"To be quite honest, I really don't. But the night is young, so why don't you humor me."

"Last night, I had that hoe squirming and willing to do anything that I wanted her to do. And it was all because of a similar line that I recall you using back on me that night you met that rapper here in the restaurant.

"Ok," Tammy said, clearly confused. "So why are you talking crap about hating me instead of praising me for giving you the knowledge you needed to handle your fucking business?"

"Because it made me wonder what the hell you're doing running those kinds of lines on me," he replied bluntly.

"Excuse you," she asked with much attitude. "This is really the shit I have to deal with after being gone so long? I should have just stayed where the fuck I was at if I would have known I was coming back to this bullshit."

She took her napkin out of her lap and threw it on the table. She hailed the waiter down and let him know that she wanted to pay for her check.

K.Y took a deep breath. "I'm sorry," he said. "I guess I just got a little carried away. It just felt weird saying that when I knew I wanted nothing to do with her when this was over. For a second, I just felt like maybe I was getting played too."

"Oh, please spare me and cut the victim shit. Here I am, giving you wisdom and getting you on your feet, and this is how you fucking re-pay me? Do you think I honestly don't have other shit I could be doing besides listening to your ungrateful ass whine about feeling played? It seems like you've got short-term memory because you've forgotten all of the headaches you've cost me since I started dealing with you."

"I know. I know. I said my bad. Look, I'm just happy that you're finally here, and I don't want to spend our time together arguing, so let's just start over."

"Uh-huh," Tammy replied. "I guess so, but cut the shit because I'm really not in the mood. How did last night go with that Spanish broad?"

"Last night went perfect, and she agreed to go with the plan just like I thought she would. Hopefully, I'll be counting my money, weighing my product, and getting you your diamond ring back real soon," he said optimistically.

"I'll have to see it to believe it. I know I said that sometimes you just have to charge it to the game, but damn this is getting out of control now," Tammy replied.

"Well, believe this," he said, pulling out another baby blue Tiffany's box from his pocket. He set it down next to him. Even though she had just been pissed off with him, the proud smile she was wearing proved that she wasn't angry anymore. "Before you open it, I want to give you this," he said as he handed her a gold key with a heart keychain encrusted with lots of gorgeous diamonds.

"What is this key for," she questioned.

"It's for our new condo. I bought it a few weeks ago. I've just been waiting on you to decorate it and hook it up so you can come home when you're ready." Next, he handed her the box. "You have to know how serious I am to have done this twice," Kyle declared as he nervously watched her, waiting for her reaction. She slid the 3.5 karat upgraded ring he bought her on her ring finger and asked, "So when can I move in?"

***

The massive three-bedroom condo he purchased was hectic with all of the moving boxes and movers hauling in the expensive furniture Tammy had purchased. She seemed to really love just standing around barking orders at people while her home was set up exactly as she wanted it to be.

"I have a guy coming in a little bit from PTJ Security Systems," Tammy declared to K.Y in between her rants to her help. "I just wanted you to know that I gave him the OK to be in here hooking up the surveillance videos."

Ever since the break-in into her last apartment and they began to put the plan to rob Ra in motion, K.Y had become overly cautious and protective.

Just as K.Y was getting ready to respond to Tammy, he noticed a call coming in from Isabella.

"Hey beautiful," he answered his phone like he always did for her. "What's up?"

"Nada papi," she replied. "I just really miss you. You've been like a ghost on me this last month. How you went from being in bed with me every night to where things are? Now, I have to schedule appointments just to see you and shit?"

Even though Tammy clearly didn't mind when he talked to Isabella, he still felt like it would be disrespectful to entertain the conversation with her present. He nodded to her to let her know that he had heard her. Then, he excused himself as he went to their outside patio that overlooked the city of Orlando to finish the rest of the call.

"It's not like I like things being this way," he lied. "I would love to be laying up next to you again, but we've got business to take care of. Don't you miss me being able to afford nice gifts for you and take you shopping and shit? I really need to recoup what I've lost so that I can continue to do that shit for you."

She sucked her teeth. "I know shit has to be done, but this is getting ridiculous," she whined.

"Cut the shit," he replied firmly. He noticed that Isabella seemed to love it when he talked to her rough. "I don't want to hear any more fucking whining. Won't it be better to enjoy a nice relaxing vacation off of some exotic beach while I'm fucking you in any position that you want me in?" Kyle asked her as he took a seat and lit his blunt.

"Wel,l if that's what the reward was, you should have said that a long time ago," she replied with what sounded like a smile. "He has two trap houses, but tomorrow night he is going to re-up at the one he has on Mercy Drive. I know the exact location and the time, so what do you want to do," she asked.

"Let's do it," he replied.

CHAPTER THIRTEEN

K.Y sat impatiently in the all-black '97 Eddie Bauer Ford Expedition a few blocks down from where Ra was getting ready to re-up.

"Here," Tammy said as she handed him the bottle of Remy. "Take a few sips of this. Just try to relax and make sure you're the one calling the shots at all times."

"I know what I'm doing," Kyle tried to assure her. "This is not my first time doing this, you know."

"Oh really," she responded sarcastically. "You sure could have fooled me with the way you're shaking like a stripper over there."

"This was supposed to be my boy. This makes this whole situation different. We used to get money together, and now I'm about to go take this nigga's shit or worst," Kyle briefly thought back to how quickly a robbery could turn deadly.

"When will you learn that in this game, you don't have any fucking friends? You took care of this motherfucker for how long? That son of a bitch didn't even come give you a single dollar or say thank you the moment he started making money off of your shit! The bastard thinks you're fucking with Isabella. But he's letting her come over here with a group of his boys to do what? Get real, Kyle! When are you going to wake up?

Why do you think I'm always preaching to you to stop putting so much trust, faith, and expectations on men? That motherfucker is human, just like you and me. There is only one person that you can genuinely believe that will never leave you or forsake you," she said before she took a big swig of the Remy straight from the bottle.

"Anyway, I've got men on both ends of the street," Tammy

continued. "Use this phone instead," she handed him a cheap prepaid. "When it rings, that means everyone is in position and ready to move. If it goes off again any other time after that, get out of that motherfucker as fast as you can. I'm going to be at the house. Call me as soon as this is over."

"That's it? What happened to the rest of the planning?"

"Really, Kyle," she asked. "I thought you said you've done this before. Shit like this does not get planned because it's the ones that over plan that get stuck when an unknown variable enters the equation." She handed him a black duffle bag. "Your mask, gloves, and SKS are in the bag. The only thing you need to worry about is getting in there, maintaining control, and making those fools fear you. You get in and get out and make sure you make it out of there safe and alive," Tammy said sternly as she looked him dead in the eyes. She grabbed his iPhone and the rest of her belongings so she could leave. "He's not your friend anymore; he's now the competition and your enemy. What do I always say about how we handle them?"

"We don't just win; we crush them," he replied, reciting one of her favorite lines.

"That's right, baby." She blew him a kiss, quickly got out of the truck and scurried to her rental vehicle before she sped off.

***

K.Y sat in the same position for five minutes until he got the call he was waiting on.

"There are five in the house if you include the runner and the girl who is ready to move," the deep voice said before it disconnected the line.

K.Y quickly drove a couple blocks over to his destination and parked the vehicle a few houses down. One of Tammy's men got in the driver's seat. "I'll be right in front as soon as you get out," he assured K.Y.

Four of Tammy's men and K.Y quickly moved to the side of the house, where they would be out of sight to anyone in the house. K.Y. briskly put on his gloves and mask then gave her the signal that they were ready to move.

Just like he had instructed her to do, Isabella went to the door and knocked.

"Who is it," the voice on the other side of the door asked.

"It's me, Bella," she replied back. "I'm here to see King,"

"He's busy right now. Bring your ass back later," the voice said firmly.

"Oh hell no," she replied. "I did not drive all the way down here for this bullshit! You better get King and open this damn door because he knows I can, and I will show out," she said much louder with a bang on the door.

Not wanting any attention brought to them, the man quickly opened the door to let her in.

"Bitch, hurry up and get your loud ass in this damn house." Before he had a chance to close the door, the young man found himself looking down the barrel of K.Y's fully loaded SKS. The rest of the men he was with quickly filed into the house with their weapons locked and loaded.

"You know what it is," K.Y said hard-heartedly. "Don't pull no crazy shit, and I won't have to let go of all 30 of these rounds that I got in this motherfucker."

The men that Tammy had hired to help K.Y had subdued their victims and tied them all up with lighting speed. They emptied their prey's pockets of any money or jewelry they had on them. Once they were satisfied with what they had, they ransacked the rest of the small house to take anything else of value with them.

K.Y walked over to the table where the transaction was taking place and swiftly swiped all of the contents into his duffle bag.

One of the men who came in with him walked over to Rashard and took the duct tape off his mouth.

"Where is the rest of the shit," the man asked with a thick island accent.

"I'm not telling you shit," Ra retorted as he spit on the man's shoe.

K.Y's accomplice took the butt of his pistol and violently struck him several times.

"Well, if you not talking, then I guess there is no point for you to even be here." The moment Ra heard the bullet enter the chamber, he quickly had a change of heart.

"It's in the floor under the kitchen table," he screamed out. "Just don't kill me, man."

One of the other men went and hastily retrieved what he went in search of.

"Jackpot," the man screamed out.

In less than three minutes, they were satisfied with all they had.

They were able to clean out Ra's stash, the products he was buying, and the money he was using to re-up.

All six of them quickly filed into the vehicle that was outside waiting for them. Once the last one was in, the driver floored the truck and speedily got out of there.

K.Y was still pumped up with adrenaline when he made the call to Tammy. "It's done," he said confidently through the phone.

"Great," she responded. "The driver already knows what hotel to take you to. Tell my men that the person who hired them will promptly pay them. Any jewelry or valuables they found are theirs to keep. When you make it to the hotel, have Isabella go into room 306. The door will be ajar, but just make sure it's locked when she leaves. Give her all of your bags, product, and weapons, and tell her to leave them in the closet. There, she will find a suitcase full of clothes for you and her for your trip to Puerto Rico. Isabella's car is parked directly in front of the hotel room, and as soon as you two get out, my men are instructed to leave. I picked out a few really sexy pieces for Isabella, and I'm sure she is going to love it."

"Wait," K.Y interjected.

Before he had a chance to say another word, Tammy spoke up to rudely cut him off. "Not now, Kyle," Tammy commanded. "You're supposed to look like the boss here, so you don't want them to hear us arguing. You do what the fuck I just instructed you to do."

She softened her tone and then continued. "I'm proud of you for finally following directions and holding your own. Please don't disappoint me now. Anyway, I'll make sure to make it worth your while when you return from vacation. You've been working very hard, and I think you really deserve this. Oh," Tammy exclaimed. "When you fuck that broad, you better use protection, or I won't let you touch me ever again. Ciao," she purred before she abruptly disconnected the call.

***

The week he had spent in Puerto Rico with Isabella turned out to be pure hell. Even though Tammy had given him permission to have sex with her, K.Y just didn't feel right being intimate with anyone besides Tammy.

"You fucking pussy," Isabella whispered to him throughout the entire plane ride home. "I hate you, and I hope your limp dick falls of for fucking with me."

While she drove her car to drop him off that evening, she could not stop talking shit and used that time to curse him out in both English and Spanish.

"I'll call you," he said as he got out and grabbed his bag.

"Don't bother, puta," she screamed out before she sped off.

K.Y got upstairs and was happy to see that Tammy had prepared a feast for him. She was wearing nothing but some red bottoms and red lipstick.

"Hey," Tammy exclaimed with much excitement. "I'm glad you're home; I actually missed you."

She gave him a huge hug and kiss and pressed her soft, warm, naked body against his. K.Y. was immediately turned on by her sudden amount of love and affection towards him and feverishly moved his hands around her well-toned body. She pushed him up against the wall and started kissing and licking him on his neck while she ran her fingers down his muscular chest.

"I've been dying to make love to you," he whispered.

She tersely stopped, lightly slapped him, and said, "I don't want you to make love to me. I need you to fuck me. Grab my hair, bite me, give it to me hard and deep," she said with much authority.

"But first, you need to eat cause you're going to need all the energy you can get. I'm about to wear your ass out," she said with a wink. "Your bath water is nice and hot. Eat quickly, so it doesn't get cold. I'll be waiting for you in the bedroom. And don't take too long," she warned him. "Because then I'll be forced to start the show without you."

K.Y. inhaled his food and was soaking in the tub in a matter of minutes.

"Damn, babe," Tammy called out from in the kitchen. "Did you even chew your food," she joked as she cleaned up his mess from the table.

Suddenly, there was a loud thud and a brief yelp from Tammy before she eerily went silent.

K.Y. jumped out of the tub, dried off, and put on his white tee and basketball shorts. He grabbed his pistol off of the counter and headed towards Tammy, and the commotion.

As soon as he opened the door, he was hit with a blunt object on his head which momentarily dazed him. The man who attacked him drug his body to the dining room area, sat him in one of the chairs, and securely tied him to the chair with duct tape as his partner had done to Tammy.

Unexpectedly, a tall, burly man wearing a ski mask and hoodie exited the master bedroom and joined them in the room where K.Y and Tammy were being held hostage by the other masked gunmen.

"Where is it," the man asked in a strong British accent.

He waited a second for one of them to squirm or point him in the direction of what he was looking for. However, when they remained utterly still and quiet, the man then became irritated.

"Where the fuck is the drugs, money, and guns," he asked angrily. "Someone better start talking soon because, in a moment, I'm going to stop being so nice," he warned them.

He walked over to where Tammy was sitting and placed the cold steel of his gun against her warm skin. The feeling instantly gave her chills as she starred into the masked man's eyes.

He took the duct tape off of her lips. "Be a doll, and tell me where I might be able to find what I'm desperately searching for."

"Fuck you," she replied back hatefully.

The man threw his head back in a wild fit of laughter. "Why don't I just fuck you," he suggested. "I'll just let your loverboy here watch while I fuck the hell out of you."

K.Y became enraged and started squirming in his seat.

"Don't tell him shit, baby. If this motherfucker thought he was coming up in MY crib for a damn thing, he is in for a rude –." Before she could finish, he used the back of his hand to slap Tammy.

"Bloody hell," he said with much annoyance. "How do you tolerate all of that blasted rubbish?" He quickly untied Tammy from the chair, grabbed a fist full of her curly hair, and pulled her head back.

"You'd have to be mad or barmy to watch me beastly bang your bitch" he said before he lifted the mask just slightly above his lips and violently forced his tongue down Tammy's throat.

K.Y noticed a small tear forming in Tammy's eyes, but she shook her head and gave him a look to let him know not to speak.

"Well, alright then," the man spoke up as he used his free hand to unbuckle his belt and unzip his zipper. He took his massively large dick and slapped Tammy across the face with it.

"Blow me," he demanded.

"Over my dead body," she retorted.

"Well dear," he said. "That could be arranged if that's really what you fancy."

Once his dick was hard, he picked Tammy up with ease and forced himself inside of her.

"Ow," she screamed out clearly in agony.

"What's the matter love? Haven't been shagged like this in a long time huh," he asked again laughing like a mad man.

"Please don't do this," she gently cried out.

The man didn't bother to respond to her plea, and instead continued to pound into her harder and deeper with each thrust.

K.Y watched on in agony as Tammy's cries went from pain to what looked like pleasure as the man had his way with her.

After a few moments, K.Y could no longer sit back and watch this show. Once one of the masked men realized that he was ready to talk, he took off the duct tape and gave him a chance to speak.

"All of the product is in the ceiling in the master bedroom closet. The money is in the mattress, and the guns are under the bed. Now, put her down and get the fuck out."

"Was that so hard," the man asked as he gently placed Tammy down on the chair. He got close to her and whispered something in her ear. Although K.Y didn't hear what the man had told her, he noticed that Tammy's eyes were in pure surprise by whatever he shared.

The other masked men retrieved the items from where they were hidden. "Cheerio mates," the burly masked man called out before he casually strolled out of their condo.

***

As soon as the men had left, Tammy grabbed a small overnight bag and packed a few of her belongings.

"Where are you going," K.Y asked.

"I can't stay here. Look what the fuck just happened. I already don't feel safe, and the fact that the asshole broke our front door isn't going to help me sleep soundly tonight. How many of your cronies know where we live," she asked while she continued packing her bag.

"The only one who knew was Isabella and Keisha," he said.

"You mean the girl you just fucked and took on an expensive vacation and the girl you've been playing mind games with for almost a decade?"

"Keisha put the place in her name so I wouldn't have to, and I never even touched Isabella like that."

"You never cease to amaze me, Kyle," she said as she finally stopped moving around and looked him in his eyes. "You were supposed to fuck her and get in Keisha's good graces! You got Keisha to put this nice as place in her name while keeping her ignored in the hood. And Isabella is probably pulling her hair out in aggravation of being used and lied to. Ugh," she screamed out. "I just need to get out of here. I'm going to be at the Ritz Carlton if you need me."

***

As soon as Tammy left, K.Y instantly hit the streets to see if anyone knew who had robbed him. After he had a moment to think, he thought one of the two women he had been toying with could have set him up as payback for fucking with their feelings. Kyle didn't go home for two days but had the door to the condo fixed the very next morning. As soon as he was sure it was safe for her to return home, he called Tammy, and to his surprise, she not only answered but agreed to check out of the hotel.

"I'll be putting in overtime to get back what all that we lost," he said to her over the phone. "I'll be home in the morning. I promise you I'm not going to quit until I find and kill whoever did this. I love you."

Although she never responded when he shared his feelings, he always wanted her to know exactly how he felt about her.

***

Just as he promised, K.Y returned early the next morning. He found it a little strange that he didn't smell his breakfast being made as soon as he walked in, but he knew that she might have still been under a lot of stress and didn't immediately see it as a cause for concern.

He walked into the bedroom and noticed that the bag she had packed the night she left was back, and everything seemed to be in its place.

After three hours went by, and he still had not heard or seen Tammy, K.Y knew something was wrong. He decided to playback the video surveillance to see what happened when Tammy returned to the apartment that morning.

He enjoyed a bowl of cereal and relaxed on the lazy boy as he watched the footage from the big screen in the living room.

He watched Tammy come into the house and put her keys on the kitchen counter like she always did. Then, she went into the bedroom,

133

placed her bag down, and got a piece of paper and a pen from their nightside table. He watched her sit down on the bed and feverishly start writing. Sometime into whatever she was writing, he saw her become emotional and start crying. When she was finished, he watched her take the piece of paper, kiss it, fold it up, and placed it underneath her key on the kitchen counter.

Scared for the worst but hoping for the best, K.Y hastily got up from his seat to retrieve what she had written.

Dear Kyle,

I don't know where to begin this letter. I don't know if I should start by saying that no matter what issues, fights, troubles, or obstacles we went through, I will forever be grateful for you and the love you've shown me. It's because of you I realized that real love does exist, and it's not just some made-up bullshit storytellers use to give us humans a sense of false hope. Maybe, I should start this off by telling you that regardless of what you think based off of my actions, this really does hurt me more than it will ever hurt you. You're an amazing man and the love you give is remarkable. In return, you deserve to be loved by someone who is capable of showing you the same. I wish it were me, but to stay here and go through all of this would mean that I would have lived my life as a lie.

No matter what happens. Always stay true to who you are.

I'll love you always,

Tee

***

Kyle eagerly paced the floor as he repeatedly tried to get through to Tammy on her cell phone. After at least the 30th time, he was surprised to hear a recording tell him that the number he was trying to reach had been changed or disconnected.

He had no idea where to go or what to do to find Tammy and make it right, but he was determined to get the love of his life back home and in his life.

Just when he put his phone down, he noticed a call coming in from a blocked number. He answered immediately.

"Hola hijo de puta," Isabella greeted him. "What happened to hitting me up?"

"FUCK YOU," he screamed into the phone. "I'm not in the mood to deal with this bullshit right now."

"I heard what happened to you and your bitch the other night," she chuckled. "Even though you pissed me off, I really don't think you deserve to have gone through that."

"What do you know," he asked.

"Everything you want to know," she replied with a titter. "This time though we are playing by my rules. Stay close to your phone. I'll call you when I'm ready to talk," she said in her attempt at a British accent before she disconnected the line.

CHARGE IT TO THE GAME 2: TAMMY'S STORY
COMING SOON

2013

Kyle Cole sat in his new, spacious, and lonely condo, thinking about the one thing he had been trying so desperately to forget – Tamia Santiago.

It had been four months since she decided to leave him and the life they shared, but the pain he still felt made the breakup feel like it had just happened yesterday.

When she packed up and left, she didn't even have the decency to tell him she was leaving to his face. Instead, she wrote him a short and sweet letter and took nothing but the clothes on her back before he made it home in the morning like he told her he would.

Since she had been gone, all of their communication was brief. When he was finally able to get a hold of her, thanks to a number he got through her old bank job, he called her twice to check up on her. She had retired from the street life and was no longer getting financial support from anyone else, so she found out just how tough life really was. He had never told her that he had a secret stash put away in case of emergencies, and he had sent more than half of the $60,000 he had saved away to help get her back on her feet.

He knew it was only a matter of time before he became stronger than he was, so he didn't think twice about sending her so much.

He grabbed the letter she left him and battled the decision to re-read her words one last time. Her penmanship was impeccable, and the letter still smelt like her favorite perfume.

Suddenly, there was a gentle knock at his door. K.Y took it to be one of his boys and decided to just let the knock go unanswered, but

136

then the gentle taps became louder and louder.

"Whatever you have, I don't want it," he screamed out.

Once he responded, and the person on the other side of the door knew he was home, their knocks became more incessant.

K.Y. finally decided to go to the door to find out who it was. When he looked through the peephole, the woman on the other end seemed very familiar. Still, he just couldn't remember where he had seen this beautiful woman from before. As much as he did not want company, his curiosity had to figure out who this woman was.

The striking and well-shaped woman immediately walked in the moment he opened the door.

"I'm sorry but do I know you," K.Y asked. He didn't even bother to hide his aggravation of this stranger just inviting herself into his home.

"I guess it is a little weird to see me fully clothed," she chuckled. "The last time we met, the only thing you saw me in was my red bottoms."

"Mrs. Carter," he asked to make sure that he had correctly identified the name with the face.

"Please just call me Josie. I'm glad I didn't have to go through the full demonstration to make sure you remembered," she replied seductively.

The thought of this gorgeous woman standing in his home naked made K.Y hard.

"From the looks of what is going on in those basketball shorts, I guess you wish you would have just waited for it," she giggled. "If you play your cards right, we might still be able to make that happen."

K.Y became embarrassed that the woman knew how excited she had just made him. It had been months since he felt the warm embrace of a woman sexually. There was no possible way to be discreet about his current erection.

"I hope you don't take this the wrong way, but why are you here? I met you once two years ago, and I never saw you again after that. What made you come check me out now," he asked.

"You and I share a common interest in a mutual friend. I want her."

The thought of Tammy instantly caused him to go soft. Although this woman was his type, she could never be the woman that he was still in love with.

"Well, as you can see, she is no longer here. You're too late," Kyle grumbled as he finally took a seat on his comfortable leather lazy boy recliner.

"I gave you some time before I came over here because I expected you to be over her by now, but it's obvious that you are not." She replied before walking over to his couch and taking a seat herself.

"Well, she's a single woman now, so she's all yours. I still don't understand why you would come bothering me for a woman that is no longer mine anymore."

"Contrary to your belief, she is not a single woman, and that is exactly why I'm here. When she was here with you, she was not a threat to me and my relationship. Now that she is no longer with you, I have a huge problem on my hands."

K.Y was instantly confused. He had worked desperately for almost a year to get the attention of Tammy, and he knew that with the love they had shared, there is no way she would just run off and be with someone else already.

"Look, lady, I have no idea what you're talking about, and I don't care to find out about your problems. Now, if you don't mind, I would appreciate it if you would get out of my house."

"Aw. I know going through a breakup is not easy, but if you were smart enough, you would have figured out by now that Tammy was not only a problem for me," she declared. "I really thought you would have figured out by now the kind of person you had been dealing with all of this time."

"I don't know what your issue is with her, and I don't care to know. If you insist on staying in my house, then the least you can do is show the woman some respect. The moment you try to play her again, you are out of here," he growled.

The woman instantly began laughing so hard that you could see tears falling from her eyes. "Please stop. Your jokes are so amusing. I can't handle it anymore," she replied while trying to catch her breath from laughing. "I understand that love is blind, and you are young, but you can't possibly be as stupid as you are making yourself appear at this moment." Josie took a few moments to pull herself together before she was able to continue. "I really do not mean to be so rude, but I just assumed I would be walking into a whole different situation. Sadly, the woman you are still in love with is not who you think she is at all. She played me, but she undoubtedly played the hell out of you."

"How the hell do you figure that? You don't know a damn thing about me."

"I do know that when you two met, you were running shit down here in Orlando. Now, look at you; instead of being out to get your revenge, you are moping around foolishly in this apartment."

"Look, we all have to take a loss to be a boss. I took some losses, but things are not over for me. She didn't leave me high and dry. I understand why things wouldn't have worked out. She wanted to go legit, and who am I to stop her."

"Please don't cause me to start cracking up in here. That girl hasn't been legit in years, and there is no turning back for her now. You've been doing your thing all this time, so do you honestly think you could ever be 100% legit ever again?"

"No, I don't, but she and I are two different people. That's the reason why we couldn't be together. I love this game, and I can never give it up. She's been in the street life all of her life, and now she's tired of it. She doesn't want to lose anyone else she loves to these streets, so she made the decision to go her separate way."

"Wow! I always knew that girl was a good ass actress, but I had no idea just how good she was. She hasn't been in the streets all of her life. She grew up in the suburbs, for crying out loud."

"I don't believe you and a single thing you're saying. I knew that woman for over a year and a half, and she let me get to know her in ways that she didn't even let her family get to know. I don't want to get nasty with you, but I will if I have to. Please excuse yourself before I get to that point."

"In your eyes, she was a huge-time drug dealer, but did you ever see her handle the product herself? Besides the sale she did with me, did you ever see her make that kind of money that fast ever again?"

K.Y didn't want to believe anything this woman was saying. It took him so long to get to know her, and he knew the kind of woman Tamia was. She seemed legit, and there was no way he could allow this woman to drag her name through the mud any longer.

"Get the fuck out. You don't know what you're even talking about. You come in my house dressed like the whore you are, and you just couldn't wait for Tamia to leave so you could try to sew your oats over here too."

"Please don't flatter yourself. I'll get out, but you know deep down there is a part of you that is curious to find out if what I'm saying is true. Put on your shirt and shoes and come with me."

K.Y had enough of taking orders from people, and Tamia was the only woman he ever allowed to tell him what to do.

"I'm not doing shit unless you learn how to talk to me properly. You came over here, so you must need my help for whatever you're trying to do. Learn some respect and how to talk to a man when you're dealing with me. Now ask me nicely," he said sternly.

"The last time I met you, I couldn't get you to say a word. I have to admit that this side of you is rather is sexy," Josie said while running her hands down her thick thighs. "Can you please get ready and come with me," she asked nicely.

"That's better. Go to your car and wait for me; I'll be down in 10 minutes."

"I don't have that kind of time, so if you're coming with me, then you need to come now."

"What the hell did I just say to you? Take your ass downstairs and wait. If you can't wait, then leave. If you leave, then forget you know me and my address and never bring your ass over here again."

For a year and a half, K.Y had been used to taking orders, so it felt good to be in charge of everything again.

"I'll be right in front of the building. Please do not take too long because we are on a time limit, and I don't want you to miss your shot at a chance of the truth," she said, sounding very sincere.

K.Y. didn't need 10 minutes, but he didn't want to let her feel like she had any control over him. He put on his shirt, jeans, a light jacket to protect him from the brisk January air, shoes, and grabbed his piece before locking up and heading downstairs. Just as she said she would, Josie sat right in front of the building in her all-black 2013 Audi S6

K.Y couldn't lie, this chick was fine, but he didn't like the way she was dealing with him. She had to be at least 5'5 without her heels on. She had a beautiful light honey complexion but was built like a video model, so it left him to wonder what her ethnicity was. Her caramel brown hair was long and flowed all the way down to the middle of her back. Her hands were the only sign that this woman was a little older, but she still looked better than most women half of her age.

"If she's so bad, then what do you want with her, and how long have you supposedly known all of this," he asked once he was settled into the vehicle.

"I've known her for years, and we haven't always seen eye to eye.

We ran in a similar circle a few years ago, so it made doing business impossible at one point. We agreed to make a truce three years ago, which is why I didn't think anything of it the time she came by my business. She knew that if anyone could help her get rid of her product fast, it would be me."

"I still don't understand what your problem with her is."

"My children's father and I dated for 9 years. I really thought that we were going to get married, but then Tammy came along. He and I had been separated for a really long time, and they had already had a bit of history. They began spending more time together, and he began spending less time at home with the children and me. I really thought he would just get over our issues, and things would go back to normal, but you can't always help who you love. I thought helping her out would get her out of my life for good. Instead, it helped solidify her position in his life," her voice began to crack, and it became evident that she was holding back tears. "She lied to you and to me just get what she wanted. Why do they get to have it all while we live alone with the pain?"

K.Y. sat silently for the rest of the car ride. He couldn't believe everything that she was saying, and it was beginning to be a little overwhelming.

After driving for what felt like forever, they finally pulled in front of a building that he knew all too well.

"How is bringing me to Tammy's old apartment really helping to prove your point? I've been here plenty of times already, and this place is not new to me. It would only surprise me to find out that she was still living here when she told me she moved back home."

"Please just follow me. I promise if you go upstairs with an open mind, you will find out soon enough that she isn't as trustworthy as she led you to believe."

They walked up the two flights of stairs to the third-floor apartment that K.Y had been to many times before. Josie took her car keys, and to his surprise, opened up the apartment door that once belonged to the women he loved.

They walked inside, and everything that he remembered was in its exact place.

"I don't get it. I thought she got rid of this place when she and I moved into our condo together."

"This place was never hers to give up. I allowed her to stay here for about a year. She paid me rent, and I let her have free reign of the place because I was always out of town on business."

Why would she lie to me about where she lived? K.Y thought to himself.

Josie walked over to the oversized chair by the window that he and Tammy had countless intimate conversations. She lit a spliff and made herself comfy on the leather chair.

"She lied to me about where she lived, and I don't understand why, but this still doesn't prove your point about her being a terrible person."

"Why would she need to lie to the man she loved about the place she called home. You guys loved each other, right? So wouldn't you need to know where to be able to locate your woman if she was ever in some sort of danger or trouble?"

"I get where you are going with this, but her father also made sure that she was well taken care of out here."

Josie sat up and looked at K.Y with a puzzled look on her face. "Now I wonder how a dead man can manage to take such good care of his little girl from his grave."

"I can assure you that he is not dead. She communicated with him weekly, and she even had a family friend vouch for her. So please find a different angle."

"Delino Santiago died four years ago," she said as she walked over to her computer table. She dug through a few files before finally finding the document she was looking for. She handed him an obituary that seemed to prove everything that she was saying about Tammy's father. Josie handed him another photo that showed Mr. Santiago in his casket with Tammy at the podium next to it.

"Then why would she have a contact under her phone as 'Papi'? One of her family friends was very protective over her because he said that he promised her father he would look out for her and keep her safe."

"Jason promised him that four years ago while Mr. Santiago was on his death bed. I had no idea why their bond was so close, but I always tried to be understanding to it, hoping that he would see that no matter what, I would love him and would be there."

"This doesn't make sense. He made it seem like this man was still alive."

"I'm not sure why he would have done that to you, but I can assure you that Delino Santiago is dead. Tee is Hispanic and we sometimes tend to call our men 'papi', so that could explain the contact in her phone. I can promise you that they have been involved together for at least 5 years. I use to have a picture of the two of them together at his funeral before I learned that they were an item and destroyed the image," she said. "He kept a contact in his phone as 'princess,' and I always thought that was for our eldest daughter, but it was for her. I really thought that man was not capable of knowing what love really was, but he's treated her so much different than I've seen him act with any woman before."

K.Y paced back and forth while he tried to go over all of the information that Josie had just given him. "You're a hating bitch, and you haven't shown me anything that really verifies anything you've said. I never met her father, so I don't know what the man looks like, and this could be fake," he said, throwing the obituary back at her. "Now hurry up and take me home before I snap and say something I'll later regret."

Josie got up from her chair and walked over to the clearly hurt K.Y.

"I know this is a lot of information, and your love for her makes everything I'm telling you hard to believe, but I need you to trust me." She grabbed his arm and led him over to the same chair she was just sitting in. Then, she guided him down into the seat and gently sat on top of him. "I don't have any reason to lie to you. Even though I was instantly attracted to the both of you, I stayed away because I sincerely wanted the two of you to work. I could tell that you loved her even from that one meeting we had. I really thought she felt the same way because you were the first person in her personal camp that I ever met. I've heard many things about you from doing my research on you first, and I know that you didn't deserve the treatment you got. I just need you to be patient with me, and I promise you that I can show you everything better than I can tell you. A man like you deserves so much more than you received, and you should at least know the truth about the woman that deceived you into falling in love with her."

After all of this time, what would this woman get for lying to me? Kyle thought to himself as he began to find comfort in her touch. He wanted to doubt everything that was coming out of her mouth, but he wouldn't be honest with himself if he didn't admit that he had already had some doubts about Tammy. For example, he spent many sleepless nights wondering why she refused to allow him to meet the man that seemed to be so important to her. In fact, it had been the start of a few arguments

***

"It just doesn't make sense to me is what I'm getting at! You say you love me and you're wearing the ring I gave you, so why can't I meet the man? I wanted to do things the proper way by asking for your hand in marriage before proposing to you, but you wouldn't even let me do that," Kyle yelled out to Tammy.

"I don't know who the fuck you think you're screaming at, but you better lower your tone before I really get upset. You asked a simple question, and I provided a simple answer – no! You just have to trust me that it's just not a good idea. If I were just one of your birds that you were used to, that would have worked, but you'll honestly be doing way more harm than good," Tammy replied.

"I'm going to have to meet him eventually, so I don't get why I can't do it ahead of time. I'm a grown-ass man, and I can handle anything that some guy throws at me."

"That's really cute, but I promise you that you have no idea who you are dealing with. If my old man was just some regular guy, then I would have set this meeting up a long time ago, but I can promise you that he's not. I already know that the moment he knew what was going on, the wedding would immediately be off.

I love him, and I refuse to be defiant on his wishes, and I know he wouldn't want me to get married. It's just that easy."

"So then what are you going to tell him once it actually happens," he asked her.

"*If* we get married, he would have no choice but to accept it.

He and I are a lot alike in certain ways. Once we've made up our minds and followed through with something, we understand that there is no point in trying to persuade the other person into our personal views. If I go to him an unmarried woman, he will see to it that it stays that way.

When I was little, my father used to tell me that all men were dogs and not to be foolish enough to fall for their lies. It's a miracle I'm even considering walking down the aisle and being a bride despite all I've seen and heard, so please don't push it any further. You asked a question, and I gave you an answer. Now, please leave me the hell alone."

***

Josie handed him the spliff that she had been smoking and offered him something to drink.

"Nah, I don't think that will be a good idea. I really just need a clear mind to sort through all of this. Part of me believes some of what you're saying, but there is a huge part of me that feels like that woman was nothing but honest to me. We never hid anything from each other, no matter how much the truth would hurt. That's the shit I liked the most about shawty. She kept everything a hundred since day one."

"So you mean to tell me that you never once questioned any of those robberies you experienced while dealing with her?

From what I heard about you in the streets, that shit was so uncommon before that chick came around. You never once believed that she might have been the one setting you up all along?"

"I never once thought that. I got involved in this shit early, and she proved to me that I didn't know the game as well as I thought I did. Thanks to her, I started making some big power moves, and a lot of my business deals were smarter than they had been previously. She taught me how to rule my camp with an iron fist and even warned me ahead of time that big results would come with enormous consequences.

Once I started really making things happen, I already knew I would have to deal with some haters. Before her, I had taken losses, but she taught me how to bounce back. There were plenty of times I had thought about getting revenge on a few people, and she actually helped me follow through on a few. Then, there were certain situations when she showed me the value of just 'charging it to the game.' You win some, and you lose some, but the object of the game is to come out on top and alive. Some battles just weren't worth fighting because I realized the risks that were involved.

That woman helped me out way too much for me to really believe that she would have been setting me up at all. She was about her money, and so was I; we were a team. Why would she have a hand in the downfall of our empire together?"

Josie was hesitant to begin speaking. It was evident to anyone that heard him talk about Tee that he had clearly placed her on a pedestal.

She placed her arm around his neck and used the other hand to caress his chest. "You're right about her being about her money, but I'm sad to say that the team she was trying to build an empire with was not with you. Unfortunately, you were just a pawn who got caught up in her game of trying to make it to the top. I've watched her hustle and manipulate situations and people before. I just never thought she would do something as sneaky as this.

She used the fact that you were young and inexperienced to her benefit. You fell in love with her, which made you blind to her tricks. A real ride or die would have held you down until the very end. That woman bounced the moment things became too tough, so there was no way she was really down for you.

She knew you were a part of this kind of lifestyle when she met you, and she continued to deal with you. Then, your organization is built up and takes your largest loss ever, and then she bounces. You can't be that in love that you won't clearly see that she had a hand in your downfall."

He handed her back the spliff.

"I know that it looks bad, but she was good to me, and that is how I'll always remember her."

"I just can't believe that a woman who loved you half as much as you loved her had the heart to look you in those beautiful eyes and end your relationship. Didn't she understand the magnitude of all of the losses you've experienced in life?"

"She didn't," he replied. "She left me a letter and was gone before I had a chance to tell her she was making a mistake. She said she knew if she told it to my face, she wouldn't be able to go through with it.

I know how she is, though, and she already made up her mind and went through with her decision, so now there is no point in fighting. I just have to love her from afar."

"How dare she? She couldn't even give you a chance to try to win her heart back, but she expects you to believe that she actually loved you? The time that you two shared wasn't even worth the decency to say goodbye to your face. At least she has the decency to leave and stay gone. It would be a problem if she was still calling or accepting your calls."

K.Y couldn't hide his facial expression. Even though they didn't talk as much as he would have liked, they have had a few conversations.

"I take it by your reaction that there is some kind of communication. Well, at least your smart enough not to give her any money if she asks for it or tell her how much you have."

His silence and uneasiness confirmed to her that he was doing the exact opposite.

"This is even worst than I thought. Kyle, you have to accept the facts; she set you up. She taught you more of the game than she was supposed to and realizes that you can bounce back on your feet with the information she gave you. She is smart enough to distance herself but wise enough not to cut you off so that she can come back around and hit you up whenever you get back on your feet again. I can't believe how conniving she is."

K.Y. instantly thought back to their last conversation. Tammy was grateful for the money she sent him, but she almost seemed angry that he had withheld so much money and information from her.

***

"Kyle Cole, where the hell did you get that kind of money to be able to send it to me," Tammy asked him.

"It doesn't matter, baby. You needed it, and I had it, so you know if I have it and you need it, then it's yours," he replied, meaning every word of it.

"I just don't get it. I only needed a few dollars to make it through the month; I really didn't need over $30,000. What doesn't make sense to me is that either you are back on and started making big moves again, or you were holding back some big secrets from me when we were together. What's up? Which one is it?"

K.Y. was a little nervous to respond because he didn't expect her to react like this. "I had a few dollars put away, and I dipped into it so that you and I could be straight. I know how you feel about me being back in these streets, but I don't know any other way to survive. I was willing to try to learn with you, but you bounced, so now I'm just going to go back to what I know."

"How do you forget to tell your woman that you have that kind of money stashed somewhere? I can get 5 or 10 stacks because that's something light, but you had enough to send me 30 stacks and still have money in your pocket. That's part of the reason why we are not together now.

It's not just about you being in these streets, but you started holding secrets, and that's the kind of shit I don't like," Tammy replied. "I appreciate the money and the help you've been giving me all of this time, but I should have known taking your call was a mistake. It's hard enough to try to piece my life together and move on without finding out that it's going to be so easy for you to make moves and move on without me. I guess I always felt needed when we were together, and this just kind of showed me that you didn't need me as much as I thought you did."

"I never needed you, shawty. I love you, and there is a big difference. That love makes me want to keep you around. I'm always going to be grateful for the help and information that you've given me. Still, I'm confident in my ability to bounce back."

"I never doubted your ability to bounce back. I knew you'd be back on your feet in no time. They forgot about you on those blocks in Orlando, and it's time that you remind them what you're capable of and who they are dealing with. Even though we can't be together like that, I will always be here and be around to talk to you."

"Maybe when I'm back on, it will convince you enough to come back home where you belong."

"I didn't bounce because you're not on anymore. I bounced because the streets are your first love, and I'll always be second to that. I'm tired of the street life, and I just want normalcy. Maybe one day you'll want the same, and if I'm still around and available, then we can try to cross that bridge when we get there. But for now, we just want and need two different things out of life."

"I want normalcy too. We can achieve it together. Let's just do it. I'll get out for good, and I'll go legit."

"How can you really expect two broke people to go legit? I'm still a struggling college student, and you just sent me most of the money you had put away."

"I have another 28 stacks put away," he said. "We can use that money to help build up your business and this time be 100% legit. I'll get a job, and you can finish school."

"That sounds cute, and if I really felt like that was attainable, I would have suggested that before I left. You have expensive taste, and so do I. We're both young and don't have to rush into anything. This space can be good for us to work on ourselves, and it can help bring us closer together.

You build your empire how you want to, and I do the same from my end. If we are meant to be together, then that is precisely what will happen in the end. In the meantime, you do what you need to so that you can be good, and I'll do the same."

"I just don't get it. I'm doing everything that I think I can to get us to work, and it seems like you are giving me every excuse as to why it can't work."

"Cut the bullshit K.Y. These are not excuses. You have always been the dreamer, and I have always been the realist of our team. How will we ever be able to survive, much less plan a wedding or family, if neither one of us is on our feet?

I'm almost finished with school, and I am possibly up for a huge promotion, so I have my life together. You want me to believe that at the age of 25, you are going to give up the only hustle that you have ever really known to tag along on my business? I would have to see some serious effort from you first.

I helped you bring your empire to where it was. All the while, I was urging you to do something smart with your money or to at least invest it in a business so you wouldn't be where you are today, and you didn't do anything like that. I told you in the very beginning that I thought you were hard-headed, and the fact that you are where you are proves that to me," Tammy replied.

"When I took that leap of faith to go with you and make it known to my family, I took the risk of being cut off completely by my old man, and that was precisely what happened. I used to have thousands of dollars coming in from him monthly just because I was doing what I was supposed to be doing, and I gave all of that up just to be with you all the time. I was determined to make us work, which is why I stayed on your ass as much as I did. When you thought I was just nagging, I was doing my best to make sure that we didn't end up here.

You were stubborn, secretive, and downright sneaky at the end of the relationship, so I left. I need to see some major improvements from you before I can even think about getting back with you. Much less moving my entire life back down to Florida," she paused and softened her tone before continuing. "You think this is easy on me, but it's not. I don't have you, and now I'm back home trying to prove myself to my old man, and it's turning out to be much harder than I would have ever expected. I feel alone most of the time, and the stress of not having the same lifestyle I had before is really pissing me off

It's hard, but you know exactly what you need to do if you want me back. If I'm not worth it to you, you can just move on and go back to doing what you've spent most of your life doing. The game is not going to be good to you forever, which is why it's always best to leave the bitch while you're still in her good graces. Whenever you get your life together, you know how to reach me," and without another word, she disconnected the call

**

Josie took her hand and gently brought Kyle's down to her over-endowed breasts.

"It's not easy to get over a first love. It's even harder when you begin to doubt if that person was real to you or if you fell in love with an illusion of who you wanted that person to be." Josie said as she used her manicured fingers to caress his ear.

"I'm at least twice your age, and it still pains me to know the horrible truth. But I couldn't sit back and do nothing while Tammy got away with breaking your heart and continuing the cycle by keeping you on a short leash. I've been there with my ex, and it's clear that he taught her his same tricks because she is now using them on you.

If you ever need anyone to talk to, I'm here for you. We can get through this together instead of suffering silently alone," she said, sounding so sincere. "Just give me a little time to get together all the proof and evidence you need. You'll see that I'm being for real in everything I'm saying to you.

I know it's hard to let an hour of information from a stranger change your mind about a love that took you years to build, but I promise you that soon you will see what I'm talking about. The woman you fell in love with is a self-centered, manipulating, egotistical, and conniving woman. She planned for you to fall in love with her so that you would never be able to suspect that she was the reason for your downfall."

ABOUT THE AUTHOR

Keaidy Selmon was born in Honduras on February 8, 1989. Since then, she has spent years driving others around her crazy as she came to grips with her own reality. After being diagnosed with an array of mental disorders throughout her life, a doctor finally admitted that her ability to create intricate plots and characters was actually a gift instead of some sort of disease.

"After I was diagnosed with Bipolar Disorder and Multiple Personality Disorder, I started taking this medication that had more risks than rewards. It slowed me down, and for the first time in my life – I actually felt crazy," she says. "After an allergic reaction to the medication, my doctor suggested that I stop taking the pills and start writing again.

One by one, all of the characters that I had known personally in my head were now free to roam in the new world I had created for them. Finishing my first novel was the first time I ever felt any real sense of freedom. That was when the pain I had been through felt worth it. I no longer aimed to just be somebody because I finally loved and accepted the woman God created me to be."

When she was asked why out of all of her books she's so passionate about the Charge it to the Game series, she said, "I write to give hope to that person who will be told there is no money to be made in the passion that sets their soul on fire. I want them to know that they should never devalue their dreams to what someone else thinks it's worth. If you're trying to measure up to other people's opinions – you'll always come up short.

Your uniqueness is what makes you shine. Find your purpose, and then share your gift with the world."

Keaidy Selmon loves to hear from her readers. If you would like to contact her, visit: www.keaidy.com and use the 'contact' form